"The past is dead and done with."

"Dead and done with." Titus repeated the phrase, his eyes bleak for a moment as he looked at Alys, but then they grew contemptuous again as he said, "And yet you ran away today."

"But not far enough, unfortunately."

"So what are you going to do—leave the ship? Run away again?"

"Sorry to disappoint you, but I really don't see why I should have my holiday ruined by something as—as trivial as this. So if you don't like me being here, then I suggest that *you* leave."

"I don't run away from my commitments."

SALLY WENTWORTH began her publishing career at a Fleet Street newspaper in London, where she thrived in the hectic atmosphere. After her marriage, she and her husband moved to rural Hertfordshire, where Sally had been raised. There is always a novel on her bedside table, and she also enjoys crafts, plays bridge and attends the ballet and theater regularly.

Books by Sally Wentworth

SALLY WENTWORTH

Mirrors of the Sea

Harlequin Books

TORONTO • NEW YORK • LONDON
AMSTERDAM • PARIS • SYDNEY • HAMBURG
STOCKHOLM • ATHENS • TOKYO • MILAN
MADRID • WARSAW • BUDAPEST • AUCKLAND

ISBN 0-373-11634-9

MIRRORS OF THE SEA

CHAPTER ONE

IT ALL happened in a great hurry. The boarding-school where Alys Curtis taught closed for the summer holidays on the Thursday. With a sigh of blissful relief she loaded her belongings into her little car and travelled to her parents' home to spend a dutiful week with them before going on a long-planned walking holiday in the Lake District with some friends. But by the Monday evening everything had changed and she found herself packing, instead, to go on a cruise round the Mediterranean.

Alys sorted her clothes with inner frustration, angry at having to forgo her planned holiday and rather resentful of the moral blackmail which had been used on her to make her do it. Her great-aunt Louise, her late grandmother's younger sister, unmarried but sprightly, had rung that morning in a great panic. When Alys had calmed her down it emerged that Aunt Louise's friend, with whom she'd been going on cruise holidays for the last twenty years, had broken her ankle the day before and there was no way she could travel.

'And we're due to go on Thursday,' Aunt Louise wailed.

'Well, you'll just have to phone up the travel company and cancel,' Alys said patiently, wondering why her aunt had chosen to tell her all this instead of Alys's mother, who was her usual confidante. 'I'm sure the insurance company will give you your money back if you——'

5

'But I don't want my money back,' her aunt broke in. 'I want to go on the cruise. But I can't possibly go alone.'

Light broke in Alys's brain with dazzling intensity. 'I'm sorry, but I'm going away myself next week,' she said firmly. 'But I'm sure Mother would——'

'No, she wouldn't; you know she never goes anywhere without your father. And I know that you only have a loose arrangement to go walking with that group you went with last year.'

'It isn't loose, it's——'

'And why you should want to go to the Lake District when you could go to Turkey and Greece, I can't think,' Louise went on as if Alys hadn't spoken. 'It never stops raining in the Lake District—especially in the summer.'

'You must find someone else,' Alys cut in quickly when the elder woman paused for breath. 'It's very kind of you to ask me, but I'm not available.'

Cutting her down to size, her aunt said shortly, 'There is no one else. You must come. You know I can't drive any more and I——'

'I'll willingly collect you and drive you to the airport,' Alys offered, hoping it would be enough.

But she should have known that given an inch her aunt would still want a thousand miles. 'I have to have someone with me all the time in case I have one of my dizzy spells. You know that. I fell and hurt myself only last month,' she said querulously.

Alys hadn't known but said, 'Well, in that case, perhaps you shouldn't go. And, anyway, don't you want to be with your friend, and help to look after her? If she's broken her ankle——'

'Certainly not. Can you see me trying to lift Helen? She's three times my size. I'd be exhausted after a day.'

Adding dismissively, 'And, besides, she has a relative who's a nurse to look after her. She doesn't need me— but I need my holiday!'

And so do I, Alys thought desperately. I want the peace and quiet of the hills, I want to be out in the clean, fresh air and have all that openness around me. Not be cooped up in a tiny cabin with an irritable old lady, on a boat that's full of men and women equally as old. 'Then you must take one of your other friends,' Alys said with fierce, almost desperate firmness. 'I'm sorry, but I can't come with you.'

'Alys,' her aunt said, in a tone that filled her with foreboding, 'I hardly need to remind you that when *you* needed help I was more than willing to give you a home and the—space I think you called it, until you felt able to face the world again.'

'No,' Alys said tightly into the pause that followed. 'No, you don't have to remind me. All right, I'll go with you. You'd better give me the details.'

'Marvellous,' Louise said happily. 'You can drive up here on Wednesday morning, then we'll have lunch, and in the afternoon we'll travel down to Heathrow and spend a night in a hotel there; that's what I planned to do with Helen. I'm sure you're going to love the trip, dear. It's a very good tour company. We'll be going to Troy and Ephesus, lots of wonderful places,' her aunt told her, her voice becoming effusive now that she'd got her own way. 'I'll give you all the details tomorrow.'

A thought occurred to Alys, remote but appalling. 'Just a minute,' she said quickly. 'You usually go on the kind of cruise that has a theme and lecturers along to tell you about it, don't you? Who are the lecturers on this cruise?'

'Do you want to know now?'

'Yes, please,' Alys answered, so firmly that her aunt didn't attempt to argue.

'All right, but you'll have to wait while I get the itinerary and put my glasses on.' Alys stood patiently, gripping the phone, an icy lump of fear deep in her heart, but it melted into nothingness as her aunt read out a list of four names that she'd never heard of before. 'And the theme is Suleiman the Magnificent. Is that all right for you?'

'Yes. Yes, that's fine,' Alys replied. 'I'll see you on Wednesday.' And she put the phone down feeling rather silly. The possibility that the one man she never wanted to see again might be on the cruise was infinitesimal, especially as Suleiman definitely wasn't his field. With that fear out of the way she could concentrate on her grievance at having her own plans ruined as Alys went to tell her parents all about it.

Aunt Louise had laid on a very nice lunch and was very conciliatory, chatting cheerfully through the meal and setting out to charm Alys back into a good mood. Not that she really needed to; having decided the night before that if she couldn't avoid this trip then she might as well try to enjoy it, Alys was ready to hear about the places they were to visit and show, if not open enthusiasm, at least some anticipation for the holiday. And being in her aunt's company helped. It made Alys remember how Louise had taken her in unquestioningly when she'd needed somewhere to lick her wounds, had cosseted her until she was ready to face the world again—or as ready as she ever could be. It had been the *unquestioning* help that had really mattered; Alys had originally gone home to her parents and at first had welcomed her father's extreme anger at the way she'd been treated, but had soon found it overpowering. And her mother had been too sympathetic, fussing over Alys as if she were an invalid, incapable of doing anything for herself. And, extremely indignant on her behalf, her mother was always wanting to discuss what had happened, which Alys found unbearable. Unfortunately she was an only child so her parents loved her too much and were too partisan. After a week or so Alys had been unable to cope with it any longer and had escaped to Aunt Louise, who had thankfully taken her in without fuss or prying, giving her some peace in which to try to come to terms with her broken romance.

So now she repaid her debt to her aunt by being as cheerful and helpful as she could, reminding her to bring her pills.

'My pills?' The older woman frowned.

'For your dizziness.'

'Oh, yes, of course.'

Louise went off to the bathroom to collect them and Alys smiled after her; really she was getting quite forgetful, although she looked healthy enough with her thin, wiry figure. She must be sixty-seven or -eight now, Alys calculated. By no means really old, but old enough to have annoying physical ailments and to want the reassurance of having someone near by in case of need. Aunt Lou lived in a very beautiful period mansion that had been converted into flats, the family that had owned it for centuries being unable to afford the upkeep any longer, so that, although she lived alone, there were always neighbours to keep an eye on her while she was at home. And on holiday there had been the slightly younger and far more robust Helen, a fellow spinster with whom she had formed an unlikely but close friendship.

Thinking it strange that her aunt should seem so uncaring about Helen's misfortune, Alys offered to drive her the twenty miles or so to visit her.

'Oh, no, I spoke to her on the phone this morning. And, besides, she isn't at home. Her relative has taken Helen back to her own home because it's easier to look after her there.'

Aunt Louise's strange behaviour was even more marked the next morning when they were at the hotel near the airport. Usually she checked in at least an hour early for any plane journey but this morning she ate such an unhurried breakfast that Alys had to remind her of the time. 'Oh, but it's only five minutes from here. We have plenty of time,' Louise said serenely, and refused to be chivvied, with the result that the flight was already being boarded when they arrived.

Because of their late check-in they had no time to buy any books or magazines and had to sit at the rear of the plane, in the smoking section. Alys wasn't very happy about it and she expected her aunt to be annoyed and show it, but to her amazement, beyond insisting that Alys sit by the window, Aunt Louise accepted the situation without complaint and sat quietly in her seat.

'Never mind, dear; it isn't a long flight,' she said absently, peering out to look down the aisle.

'Aunt Lou. Aunt Louise,' Alys repeated more loudly when the woman didn't answer. 'Are you feeling all right?'

'What? Oh, yes, of course.' Her aunt sat back. 'I was looking to see if I recognised anyone, from a previous holiday.'

'You've been with this tour company before, then?'

'Oh, yes. Helen and I always go with this company. They look after you so well.'

Alys refrained from asking in that case why her aunt had felt that a companion was indispensable. She was here now and determined to make the most of the unexpected trip. When they were in the air she took out the itinerary again and felt a thrill of excitement at the prospect of seeing so many places she'd only read about. Mount Athos, Istanbul, Troy, Philippi, Knossos, Delphi, Ephesus; the names read like a scroll of history, like a book that you'd always known about but had never been allowed to open before. A treasure chest of time.

A stewardess came round offering drinks and Alys came back to earth—or rather to mid-air. Taking out a notepad, she began to map out a course of study based on the holiday, which she could use during next term's history lessons for the fourth-form girls. It would be far more interesting for them if she had slides to illustrate it and perhaps some artefacts to display. The names of the guest lecturers were at the bottom of the page, and one of them, a Professor MacMichael, caught her attention. It wasn't a familiar name; she was sure she hadn't come across him when she was at university or on a course, but she seemed to remember reading about him somewhere, and quite recently. But it couldn't have been anything very interesting because she couldn't bring it to mind; it was just the unusual name that must have caught her attention. Dismissing it, Alys carried on with her outline until lunch was brought round.

They were headed for Corfu, and, although it had been quite warm in England, when they stepped off the plane the air was at least ten degrees hotter, wrapping them like a comforting blanket. They were among the last off, Aunt Louise having dropped her glasses on the floor as she stood up, so that they had to wait to search for them. Because the plane had been a special charter, booked to carry only the cruise-line passengers, they didn't have to wait for their luggage, just went through the formality of Passport Control and then out to the waiting coaches, the first of which had already left.

Aunt Louise decided that she wanted to sit by the window this time, but as Alys looked past her at the landscape of hills and wooded valleys, saw olive trees casting a gnarled shelter for the browsing sheep and goats, she felt a strong sense of pleasure and anticipation, a true holiday feeling. Impulsively she turned to her aunt and kissed her on the cheek. 'Thanks for inviting me.'

Louise gave her a surprised glance, her eyes strangely discomfited. Perhaps she didn't like displays of affection in public. But she said wryly, 'You didn't want to come. You'd rather have gone with your friends.'

'Yes,' Alys admitted. 'But now I'm glad I'm here.'

After hesitating a moment, Louise said, 'Your friends—they were all girls, weren't they? There wasn't a young man you were hoping to see? Someone special?'

Alys shook her head. 'No, they're all girls. We went to college together.'

'That's what I thought.' Aunt Lou seemed strangely relieved. 'So there hasn't been anyone else since——'

'No,' Alys interrupted quickly. Then pointed towards the window. 'Oh, look! There's a woman on a donkey.'

Recognising the abrupt change of subject as a keep-out signal, Louise didn't attempt to bring up the past again. Alys was surprised and rather disconcerted that she had mentioned it at all; the good thing about her aunt had been her ability to accept without prying. But perhaps she had been guiltily thinking that she had taken Alys away from a new relationship by making her change her holiday plans.

The sea came in sight and soon a woman behind them exclaimed excitedly, 'There she is!' and they saw the cruise ship moored in the port. As cruise liners went it was quite small, with only five decks, the lowest on the water-line. It was painted cream and white, its one funnel blue, and looked like a sedate old lady who was well past her best but was trying hard to keep up appearances. Like most of her fellow passengers, in fact, Alys thought with an inward grin.

Their cabin wasn't exactly spacious but it wasn't as tiny as Alys had feared. Aunt Louise had splashed out on one of the larger ones on B Deck, on the port side towards the bow of the ship. There were two beds, not bunks, and it had a proper window rather than a porthole, for which Alys was grateful as it made the room feel far less claustrophobic. And there was a bathroom with a bath as well as a shower. Sheer luxury! A steward brought their cases while Alys was in the bathroom, washing, and Louise insisted that they unpack before exploring the ship.

'I'm sure it hasn't changed since last year,' she remarked. 'And I want to hang my clothes up so that the creases fall out.'

Alys obediently helped her, wondering why her aunt was now being so fussy about unpacking immediately when she hadn't bothered to unpack at all at the airport hotel last night. Their cabin was on the side away from the dock and they could only dimly hear the noise of the port, but then they felt the slight throb as the engines came to life, and when Alys looked out of the window she saw that the ship was moving out of the harbour.

'We're at sea,' she said with a smile.

Her aunt's shoulders seemed to sag in a relaxation of tension and she returned the smile. 'This is always the best moment.'

Alys hung her own clothes in the space that was left; she'd brought mostly casual clothes, those that she'd intended for her walking trip, plus some separates that she could mix and match for the evenings and a couple of snazzy numbers for the gala nights when everyone dressed up.

'Shall we go on deck?' she asked when she'd finished.

Louise pursed her lips in momentary hesitation, then nodded. 'Why not?' she said decisively. 'I should like a drink.'

Thinking she meant a cup of tea or coffee, Alys headed for the lounge, but her aunt went straight to the bar and ordered a couple of cocktails.

'I didn't know you drank this kind of thing,' Alys said in surprise as she sipped her highly coloured drink.

The older woman was looking searchingly around at the other passengers, but turned to glance at Alys as she answered cryptically. 'I expect you'll find out a lot of things you didn't know about me on this trip.'

Alys immediately had mental visions of her very respectable aunt letting her hair down, and wondered with intrigued amusement what was to come. Their drinks finished, they went for a walk round the ship to see the minute swimming-pool, the promenade deck where you could play quoits, and the observation deck that was right above their own cabin. Here they met two women whom Louise knew from a previous holiday and all three began chatting animatedly. Moving away a little, Alys leaned on the rail, watching the mainland drift by in the evening sunlight, feeling a sudden sense of sadness. It was an emotion that still overtook her at the oddest moments—a sensation of loneliness and lost opportunity, an 'if only' kind of feeling.

'Such a shame about Professor MacMichael,' she heard one of the women say, and pricked up her ears.

Louise coughed. 'Oh, really? What happened to him?'

'Didn't you read about it in the papers? The poor man was involved in that multiple car accident on the motorway last month. I believe his wife was seriously injured, too. But they've found someone else to take his place. A man from——'

'How terrible!' Louise broke in. 'Was the professor badly injured?' She moved away as she spoke and the women's voices became just a murmur, almost lost in the slap of the bow wave against the side.

The westerly breeze lifted Alys's hair, fair and as fine as silk. The deep gold of the setting sun enhanced the fine bone-structure of her face, shadowed the graceful curves of her slim, athletic body. She thought she must be the youngest person on the ship, apart from the crew of course. Most of the passengers seemed to be retired people, making the most of their leisure years, although there were a few younger couples—younger, but still middle-aged, and therefore too old for Alys.

But at dinner that evening they found themselves on a table with two women in much the same position as their own—a mother with her daughter along as companion. Alys hadn't noticed them before but it seemed that the daughter had noticed her and had manoeuvred her mother into sitting at their table. It wasn't the kind of cruise where you were given the same table for the whole trip; here the tables were filled up as people arrived, the captain and officers eating in their own quarters except on gala nights. The daughter, who introduced herself as Gail Turnbull and her mother as

Jennifer Gilbert, was older than Alys, probably in her early thirties, but was nearer in age than any of the other passengers she'd seen.

Gail seemed to be of the same opinion because, after she'd determinedly sat next to Alys, she lowered her voice and said, 'Thank goodness there's someone else on this trip who's under a hundred. I take it you're here as dutiful relative-cum-nursemaid, too.'

'I'm with my aunt,' Alys admitted, not sure whether she wanted to be drawn into a kind of instant youthful alliance against the older generation by a complete stranger.

Gail made a sympathetic face. 'Ma insists on having me go with her on these trips, then spends all her time with her cronies so that I'm bored to death. Never mind; we'll be able to keep each other company.'

She turned away as the waiter came up, giving Alys the chance to look at her objectively. With her curly dark hair and tanned skin, Gail had a gypsyish look about her, an impression heightened by her dark brows and brightly made-up lips. Lips that had a slightly pouting tilt, whether from a sulky nature or because Gail thought it looked sexy it was too soon to tell. But she was good-looking in a sultry, sensual kind of way. Men must find her so, anyway, because she wore a wedding-ring on her finger—rings on most of her other fingers, come to that, as well as bracelets and a heavy gold chain necklace.

Alys turned to talk to her aunt and they were into the main course before Gail leaned towards her confidentially and said, 'I suppose it's too much to hope that there might be any halfway decent single men on this trip. Some of the waiters aren't too bad,' she murmured, looking contemplatively round the room, 'but the trouble with the Greeks is that most of them are so short.' Her voice became more animated as she leaned nearer. 'I did catch a glimpse of one really gorgeous man—and without a grey hair in his head, would you believe?' But then she became pessimistic. 'I haven't been able to find out who he is yet, but you can bet your life he's with his wife—he's much too divine not to have been snatched up already. Have you seen him yet?'

Shaking her head, Alys laughed. 'No, I definitely haven't seen anyone I'd describe as "divine".'

'Well, you'll recognise him when you see him.' Gail glanced at Alys's ringless left hand. 'I take it you're not married?'

'No.'

'Neither am I.' Adding, when she saw Alys's surprised look, 'I'm divorced. Twice, actually. The trouble with me is that when I'm married I want to be free, and when I'm free I can't wait to get married again. Terrible, isn't it?'

Taken aback by her candidness, Alys said, 'Yes, I suppose it must be. What do you—er—do when you're not married?'

'Do? Oh, you mean for a career?' Gail laughed in surprise. 'I don't *work*. I never have. I got married the first time as soon as I left school so I didn't have to. Then I lived on alimony. And the same this time around. Just as well, really. I couldn't possibly sit in an office all day; it would be too deadly boring.' She looked at Alys. 'What do you do? Are you a model or something?'

With an inner smile of amusement, Alys said, 'Nothing so glamorous. I'm a teacher. At a girls' school. I teach history and sports.'

'How interesting,' Gail commented politely, but obviously thinking it as boring as hell. 'I don't suppose you have much chance to meet many eligible men at a girls' school?'

'Not many, no.'

'That's an awful shame with your looks and figure. I suppose it's all that sport.'

'Very likely,' Alys agreed, accepting the oddly given compliment with amusement.

Aunt Louise and Gail's mother seemed to be getting along quite well, so the four of them stayed together after dinner when they went up to the lounge for coffee. There were about two hundred and fifty passengers on board and perhaps half of them had gathered in the lounge, many of them already forming into groups around the circular tables. Alys looked round, wondering which man was the one Gail had described, but Gail, guessing her thoughts, shook her head. 'He isn't here,' she murmured conspiratorially.

Annoyed with herself, Alys turned away; she had come on this trip to please Aunt Louise, not to meet men, and she didn't want Gail to include her in her own obvious man-hunt. Just because she wasn't married didn't mean that she must therefore be hungry for male company. When you'd partaken of the best then nothing less would do. The unbidden and unwanted thought made Alys tighten her grip on her coffee-cup, and when her aunt said she was tired and was going to the cabin Alys got up to go with her, refusing Gail's suggestion of a walk round the deck.

Used to sleeping in a high-ceilinged room with the window open, Alys woke in the night feeling hot and stuffy in the little cabin. In the other bed her aunt slept soundly, very soundly! Her snuffling little snores drowned the buzz of the air-conditioning. For half an hour or so Alys tried to go back to sleep, then gave up, put on her bathrobe and slipped out of the cabin and up the nearby stairs to the observation deck. Above her there were lights in the bridge section as the crew steered the ship, but she had the deck to herself. They weren't going so fast now and the breeze hardly lifted her hair, but it was much cooler out here. There were distant lights on the land on both sides of the ship, so they must be going through the narrow Gulf of Corinth. The smell of the sea was strong in her nostrils, drowning any scents from the land. It made her remember the day she'd met Titus. That, too, had been on a boat, but a much smaller one than this, the ferry boat coming back from the Shetlands to mainland Scotland.

For a few moments Alys let her thoughts drift, remembering her first sight of him in jeans and sweater, his thick dark brown hair, worn quite long then, blown back from his face, emphasising the strong bone-structure and square jaw. He was standing with a small group of similarly clad young men at the far end of the deck, but Alys had felt his eyes on her and had turned. That incredible 'across a crowded room' bit had come true for her then. She had looked into his eyes and it was as if they were alone, there was no one else on the thronged deck, no pop music coming from someone's radio, no wind, no sea, no sky. Just the face of this stranger whom she instinctively knew was to be part of her destiny, her future.

She stood, staring at him like a fool, until someone moved between them and she couldn't see him any more. Then she flushed and turned back to her friends, expecting them to be gazing at her in amazement, as aware of what had happened as she was. But they hadn't even noticed, were all occupied in holding the map in the wind and choosing a place to stay for the night. It was some minutes before Alys dared to look again to where the man had stood, and she was devastated to find that he had gone. Perhaps it hadn't been the same for him, she thought in a panic, perhaps he hadn't been looking at her at all. Without thinking about it, she began to move towards where he'd been standing, but it had begun to rain heavily and the others pulled her inside the crowded saloon, ignoring her protests.

And then she saw him again, over by the small bar. He was very tall, taller than almost everyone in the room, and when he turned and looked round he found her almost at once. Alys almost lifted a hand to wave, sure that his eyes were searching for her. Almost—but not quite.

She waited, not knowing what to do, her heart thumping, her throat tight. Without acknowledging her at all, he faced the bar again and said something to his companions. Alys's heart crashed through the bottom of the boat, but began to soar again as the big stranger turned, shouldered his way through the crowd of passengers and came to stand in front of her. 'Hello.' The greeting was almost hesitant and there was a slightly punch-drunk look about him, a look, she realised, that must be mirrored in her own face.

'H-hello.'

For a moment they just stared at each other like a pair of fools, but then he grinned and held up the bottle and plastic tumblers that he carried. 'They didn't have any champagne—seems they don't have much call for it on a ferry, so I got the only thing they had that was fizzy. Lager. Will it do?'

Alys smiled up at him, her eyes radiant. 'Lager will do fine.'

He filled the tumblers and they solemnly clicked them together. They didn't have to say the rest; their eyes said it all.

But then they became aware of their own silence and he said, 'I'm supposed to be on a climbing holiday with some friends. Except that it's hardly stopped raining since we've been here. How about you?'

'A walking tour. But we've been soaked every day, too.'

'We're thinking of heading for the Peak District instead; the weather's supposed to be all right there.'

'Is it? I haven't seen the forecast.'

She smiled suddenly, thinking how English their behaviour was—talking about the weather when their hearts were doing crazy somersaults and a great golden glow of happiness was spreading through their veins, shining from their eyes. She couldn't believe that others couldn't see it. Surely everyone in the saloon must be staring at them in dumb-struck awe. But the noisy hubbub of voices was the same, the boat still pitched and rolled in the wind, there was the same cloying smell of dampness from people's clothes. But he understood and smiled back, this large stranger with his hair dishevelled by the wind and rain, and dressed so ordinarily in jeans and sweater, tough holiday wear.

Alys sipped her drink and looked at him over the rim. He was older than her, almost thirty, she guessed, and very good-looking in an open, strong kind of way, even though there were a couple of little lines around his mouth that betrayed his experience of life. But she took little notice of those lines, too overwhelmed by the wonder of it all to even think about his past; they were just part of the features that together had brought to life a face that yesterday she hadn't known but now would mean everything to her for the rest of her life. And he had been looking her over too, because as the ferry hooted as it approached the dock he leaned forward and quoted softly into her ear, ' "Divinely tall and most divinely fair".'

Her face was still flushed when they walked off the ferry on to the jetty together. The rain was pouring again by now but she put up the hood of her anorak with reluctance. The other girls were waiting for her, aware now that she had met someone, their eyes alive with curiosity.

'We've got a minibus,' he said, pointing to a vehicle that was being driven off the ferry. 'Why don't you let us give you all a lift?'

'Yes, *please*,' she said unhesitatingly, and so fervently that he laughed.

Taking his hand, feeling an overwhelming rush of emotion as she did so, she led him over to the girls. Excitedly she said, 'We've been offered a lift. This is——' She stopped suddenly, disconcertedly realising that she didn't know his name.

'Titus Irvine,' he supplied, mouth twitching in amusement.

'Titus,' she repeated, drinking the name in, engraving it on her heart. 'And I'm Alys.'

So they'd all crowded in the bus among the climbing gear and rucksacks, and she and Titus had sat close, covertly holding hands, full of joyous anticipation as they'd driven off into a future that could only be bright and golden after such a wonderful start.

But now Alys grimaced wryly in the darkness as the ship chugged along through the night. It had been such a romantic beginning that she'd thought it too good to be true. And she'd been right. What had started with instantaneous love and attraction had suddenly turned to stubborn, uncompromising anger, to jealousy and hate, and she had run away, unable to take it. Run to Aunt Louise—who would worry if she woke and found her gone. Determinedly pushing the past from her mind, Alys went back to the cabin, let herself silently in, climbed into bed and this time fell instantly asleep.

Alys was used to waking early to go for a morning jog before school started, and the next morning, despite her sleepless night, she woke at the usual time. To her surprise her aunt was already up and dressed.

'Breakfast is at seven this morning,' she reminded Alys. 'Have you forgotten we're leaving for Delphi at eight o'clock?'

'Have we moored?'

'Yes. We're at Itea. Come along, Alys; I know how you young people like to lie in bed half the morning.'

Her aunt's voice was chiding but there was a note of subdued excitement in it that made Alys realise how much Louise must have looked forward to this holiday, and she was really glad now that she had agreed to come.

Breakfast was a buffet-style meal which they ate quickly so that Aunt Lou could go back to the cabin and make sure she had everything she needed for the trip. Normally Alys would have worn shorts and a strapless sun-top, but, remembering the age of her fellow passengers, she put on a more sedate top and lightweight skirt. Gail Turnbull, though, had had no similar regard for age. If any of the old gentlemen had been on the verge of a heart attack they would probably have had one when they saw her walk down the gangplank in a minute pair of bright red shorts and a halter-neck top that left her midriff bare. Alys said as much to her aunt, who gave an unladylike snort of derision. 'Nonsense! It will do them all the world of good.'

Alys burst into laughter and allowed her grinning aunt to shoo her on to the first of the waiting buses.

The cruise company issued all the passengers with printed handbooks about Greece and Alys had read up about Delphi, knew that it was the home of the oracle, that there was a theatre and stadium, and a museum—closed Tuesdays—containing the famous bronze statue of a charioteer. But nothing had prepared her for the magnificent natural setting. As the coach rounded the last bend the entire horizon was bounded by mountains and in their centre a great plain that was a sea of olive trees. They stopped and alighted at Mount Parnassus where the sanctuary of Delphi was built on a steep and narrow shelf of land on the lower slopes, the sheer cliffs of the shining ones behind it, and to the south a deep ravine.

It was still very early and they were the first group of tourists to arrive that day. As soon as Alys had moved away from the bus she was aware of the peace and quietness of the place, a peace that came not from the lack of sound but from an aura of deeply ancient tranquillity. Even if there had been no ruins here she sensed that she would still have felt this inner peace. A local guide was waiting to meet them and led them to the Temple of Athena, reeling off historic facts, but Alys mostly switched off, letting the feel of the place take her over. They moved on, the other busloads of passengers duly following in their turn, but when they reached the Sacred Way where the ground rose steeply Aunt Lou said firmly that she wasn't going to climb any higher. Several others agreed with her and they sat down on the fallen stones in the shade of an old, spreading olive tree to rest.

   Confident that her aunt was in good hands, Alys went
on with the rest of their group but instead of staying
with them she hung back a little and the guide soon went
on ahead. It was magical to walk alone up the ancient
way, to see a lizard sunning itself on a fallen stone carved
over two thousand years ago, to look down on the distant
plain of olive trees and see them move like rolling waves
in the breeze, to see the butterflies, and to feel a primitive
sense of a holy presence here on the mountain. Was that
what the ancient peoples felt? Alys wondered as she
climbed higher. Was that why they came on such long
and dangerous pilgrimages and to consult the oracle?
She reached the remains of the old theatre, built to face
the distant valley, and paused to look back at the un-
believable view. But something urged her on and she soon
went past it, taking the path that led on to the long flat
plateau of the stadium. The bases of the stone archways
at the entrance were still standing and a strange feeling
of heady anticipation filled Alys as she walked between
them. To her right there were still the tiers of seats where
the spectators had sat to cheer on the contestants in the
ancient games that had been held here, but to her left
they had broken away and the view was screened by trees.
   The sun was hot now as Alys walked slowly down the
long length of the beaten earth, her shadow sharp and
black against its greyness. There was no other human
being there; not even the strident voices of the guides
carried so high. She had been no stranger to loneliness
for a long time, and easily recognised its insidiousness,
but here, even though she was entirely alone, she felt
only the warmth of an inner peace and a growing
eagerness for life. She neared the curved end of the
stadium, trying to imagine it as it had been, wishing she
could go back in time and see it then. When she reached

the very end, she turned and looked back at the entrance. She wasn't alone any more; a man was standing in the shadow of the entrance arch. As she watched he moved forward into the sun and she saw, somehow without surprise, that it was Titus.

CHAPTER TWO

ALYS blinked, expecting this sun-drenched dream, this mirage, to disappear. But Titus was still there. Really there. Not a figment of her wayward imagination. For an agonisingly long moment Alys couldn't move, was so shocked that she hardly even breathed. Titus, too, seemed to be rooted to the ground, and it was only when he stepped forward, his steps hesitant and uncertain, that Alys's limbs unfroze. She instinctively moved backwards but was brought up short by the wall of the stadium. Her body began to shake and she looked wildly round, seeking for some means of escape. But then another figure appeared in the entrance behind Titus, an unmistakably female figure in bright red shorts and halter-top.

Gail called out to Titus but he didn't appear to hear and came on, still moving slowly, as if he, too, could hardly believe his own eyes. But then Gail called again, more loudly, 'Dr Irvine.' And this time he heard, slowed, but came to a stop, looking reluctantly over his shoulder.

Alys didn't hesitate. She leapt for the side of the stadium where the seats had broken away, was over it, and scrambling down the steep hillside on the other side. There were broken stones among the trees, and she was in imminent danger of falling or twisting her ankle, but Alys didn't care so long as she didn't have to walk back along the length of the stadium to where Titus stood, didn't have to pass him with the terrible choice of having to speak or else just ignore him. Her sandalled feet slid on loose pebbles and she swayed but recovered immediately, her fitness and physical agility thankfully helping her when she needed it most. She came to a path, not much wider than a goat track, that would have led her back to the theatre, but Alys ignored it because it was in sight of anyone looking down from the stadium, instead plunging on down the hillside until she came on to a much wider path lower down the slope and nearer the main body of ruins, which she quickly ran along until she was hidden by a wall and knew that she couldn't possibly be seen.

She stopped then, leaning against the wall, trying to control her sobbing breath, which came not only from physical exertion but also from the shock of seeing Titus there so unexpectedly. How could he be here? How could he? Ancient Greece wasn't his field. But then she realised what a stupid thought that was; even lecturers in Egyptology had to take holidays, didn't they? A holiday! On the ship! Alys's heart froze again. It couldn't be. Oh, no, please not that. But he might not be on the ship; it might just be coincidence that Titus was at Delphi at the same time as their group.

Balling her hands into tight fists, Alys pressed them against her temples, trying to still her chaotic thoughts and fears, desperately trying to think logically. If he was just on holiday in the area then it didn't matter, she ... Suddenly Alys remembered Gail Turnbull. She had called Titus by his name, which could only mean that he was also a passenger on the ship. Grimly recalling Gail's description yesterday evening of a 'divine man', Alys now knew who the other girl had seen. But she shook her head in perplexity; a cruise like this wasn't Titus's scene. He was much more likely to spend his summer vacation working on a dig in Egypt than sailing the Mediterranean with a shipload of near-geriatrics. Not unless he was paid to do it.

With that thought everything suddenly fell into place. A lecturer who'd had to be replaced at the last minute, Aunt Louise's friend's so convenient broken ankle and her aunt's insistence that she couldn't travel alone, along with all the little things that had seemed odd but trivial at the time but now added up to make a very clear picture. Alys's body shook again, but this time from anger. How dared her aunt manipulate her life like this? Pushing herself off the wall, Alys strode along the path and through the ruins until she came to where her aunt still sat under the olive trees, waiting. When she saw Alys she got to her feet with a smile of greeting, but it quickly faded when she saw the fury in her niece's face.

'How *dare* you?' Alys got out, her voice trembling with anger.

But her aunt lifted her hand. 'Not here,' she said, so forcefully that Alys only then became aware of other passengers sitting in the shade and watching them with interest.

'Let's walk this way, then, shall we?' Alys put a firm hand under her aunt's elbow and led her away from the others, walking too fast for the older woman but too angry to care, leading her along a path until they came out on to a rock platform above a stream.

'This must be the Castalian Spring,' Louise remarked breathlessly, a hand to her chest.

'I couldn't care less what it is,' Alys retorted. 'And please don't try to change the subject. I'd like to know just what right you think you have to play around with my life like this?'

Louise sat down on a convenient rock, her back to the sun. 'None at all, I suppose.'

'You knew Titus was going to be on this cruise and that's why you insisted I came along. Please don't try to make an even bigger fool of me by denying it.'

'I am not trying to make a fool out of you, Alys. You know I would never do that. You are my favourite niece and I love you very much,' her aunt replied calmly.

'Then *why*?' Alys spread her hands in a gesture of despair. 'Why do you want to hurt me like this?'

'Does it still hurt so much, then—even after so long?'

Alys stared down at her aunt, the question forcing her to admit that the feelings she had tried so hard to conquer were so shallowly buried that they had immediately overpowered her the moment she had seen Titus again. She turned away, looking blindly up at the cave-strewn cliff behind them, gold in the sunlight. 'Yes,' she said huskily. 'I think it will always hurt.'

'Then don't you think——?'

But Alys had swung round. 'I don't want to discuss this. I'm going to the ship to collect my things and then I'm going home to England by the first plane.' And she began to stride back along the path.

'Coward!'

The vehemently spoken word was caught up by the cliff and echoed along the gorge. Alys tried to ignore it but it seemed to hammer into her brain. She stopped, her hands balled into fists, but didn't turn round.

'I thought you had more courage than to run away,' her aunt added shortly.

Slowly Alys turned, trying hard to control herself. 'It is not a question of running away. I already did that nearly two years ago. Now I just want to forget—forget the past and get on with my life.'

'But you're not, are you?'

Alys bit her lip. 'Please, I don't want to talk about this. I——'

'Well, I think it's high time you did,' her aunt responded stoutly. Getting to her feet, she came and took hold of Alys's arm, noticed her clenched fists. 'My dear child,' she said gently, 'look at yourself. Just seeing Titus has turned you into a nervous wreck. How can you get on with your life when your emotions are still so involved in the past?'

'Are you trying to get us back together; is that it?' Alys demanded harshly. 'Because I can tell you now that——'

'No, that was *not* my intention,' Louise said firmly. 'But I think it's high time you got Titus out of your system once and for all. But you're never going to do that unless you face up to it—face him. Unless you meet someone else and fall hopelessly in love again, of course. But that's highly unlikely while you're still brooding about the past and shutting yourself away in a girls' school. You even go on holidays with other women,' her aunt said disapprovingly.

'Being married—having a man—doesn't have to be every girl's aim in life. Not nowadays. You can have a very fulfilling life without them.' She glanced at her spinster aunt and added on a slightly malicious note, 'You should know that.'

'I suppose I deserve that,' Aunt Louise said stiffly. 'But my fiancé was killed, as you very well know.'

'But you never looked for anyone else. You never wanted anyone after him; I remember you telling me that.'

'That's so,' Louise admitted. She drew Alys back to the rocks, made smooth by countless feet, and they sat down. Behind them the spring that fed the brook burbled and sang as it splashed over the stones, as it had done for thousands of years. Apart from the stream it was very still and quiet; everyone else had gone down to the museum and they had the place to themselves. 'I was completely devastated when my fiancé died,' Louise went on. 'I grieved for him very deeply, but he was dead and nothing would bring him back. And at least I knew that we had been happy together and nothing had marred that. With you and Titus it's very different.'

Ignoring Alys's sound of protest, she went on firmly, 'You parted from Titus on bad terms, your emotions in turmoil. I don't think you've got over that.'

You can say that again, Alys thought with inward bitterness. But it had been much worse than her aunt had described. Her emotions had been raw, bleeding, after that terrible fight. So bad that she couldn't bear to stay. And once she'd left, even when she'd had time to realise how desperately she missed and needed Titus, there had been no going back. She had been too proud, too hurt, for that, and Titus far too unbending to beg her to go back to him, even if he'd wanted her, which was highly unlikely as he hadn't attempted to get in touch with her even once since she'd walked out on him, Alys remembered drearily.

'I know that it's been very difficult for you and that you've tried very hard,' Aunt Louise said. 'I saw you struggling with yourself and my heart ached for you. I hoped you would get over him in time, but I saw you cut yourself off more and more, and I knew that you hadn't. So when I received the notification that Titus was taking the place of one of the other lecturers on the very cruise Helen and I had booked for, well—it seemed a heaven-sent opportunity for you to come to terms with yourself one way or the other.'

'What do you mean?'

'You'll either realise he's the only man in the world for you, that you've lost him and that you have that to live with, or you'll find that he isn't important to you any more and that you can now forget him and start living properly again.'

'If only it were that simple,' Alys said despairingly. 'You don't know what you're asking. I can't go through with this.'

'I think you must, for your own sake. You've changed a lot since you left him, Alys. You used to be so light-hearted, so full of life. I would give a great deal to see you happy again.'

'It won't work! It will just reopen old wounds. It's over. Done with. Can't you see that?'

'I see just the opposite.' Her aunt gripped her arm. 'You have got to exorcise him from your heart once and for all. Otherwise you'll grow bitter and mean-spirited, your life ruined by your one mistake of falling in love with the wrong man. Face him, Alys. Try to look at him with your eyes and not your heart. Let him go.'

'And if I can't?'

'Then try to remember only the happy times. Hold them to your heart and let the bad times fade away. Remember the man you loved and not the man you hate. Have you the courage to do that, my dear?'

'I don't know. I may just jump overboard.'

Her aunt smiled. 'Oh, no, you're not that kind of coward; you've already proved that.'

Her thoughts going back to the weeks she'd spent at her aunt's house after she'd left Titus, Alys only now realised that Louise had never left her alone in the house, had insisted that she came and sat with her, and that the key of the bathroom had mysteriously disappeared. 'You took better care of me than I knew,' she said huskily, touching the older woman's freckled hand.

'I didn't want to lose you. I still don't—not even to bitterness.'

Alys looked into Aunt Louise's steady grey eyes for a long, long moment, then gave a deep sigh and nodded. 'All right. I'll try.'

'Good.' Louise got briskly to her feet. 'Now can we go and get a drink? I've talked myself dry!'

She began to walk back along the path to the Sanctuary and Alys fell in beside her. 'What would you have done if I'd refused to go back to the ship?' she asked wryly.

'You couldn't have done; the purser has your passport and I made him promise not to let you have it back until the end of the cruise.'

Alys gave an indignant gasp, then laughed reluctantly. 'And your friend Helen; wasn't she upset about missing her holiday?'

'No, because I've already booked for another cruise in September that we'll both enjoy.'

Something in her tone made Alys look at her keenly and then say, 'You knew I'd be angry. And you knew that I could easily make the trip unbearable for you, yet you were willing to do it for my sake.'

Her aunt nodded. 'And now I think that **you**'re going to go through with it largely for my sake.'

They came to the point where the path joined the Sacred Way and Alys braced her shoulders. 'With any luck we'll find that Titus has decided to jump ship instead,' she said sardonically.

'Is he a coward, then?'

Alys shook her head without even thinking about it. 'No, never.'

'Then he'll stay,' her aunt said with confidence.

It was a long walk down to the museum and the sun was much hotter now, so they took it slowly. Glancing back at the ruins climbing the hill, Alys knew that in future Delphi would mean only one thing to her: Titus's figure walking out from the darkness into the sun, out of the past into the present. And the future? Alys pushed that thought out of her mind. I'll take each moment as it comes, she thought. But I won't hide myself away in the cabin, much as I'd like to. I've promised Aunt Lou I'll face this and I'll keep the promise—somehow, somehow.

The museum was a modern building of cement and glass, making no concessions to the age of its artefacts or the beauty of its surroundings. Though comparatively small in size, it housed some of the most beautiful objects ever found, especially the life-sized bronze statue of a charioteer. But Alys only looked at the exhibits unseeingly, her senses on edge for any sign of Titus. He came out of the room leading to that housing the charioteer just as they were about to enter it, so that it was impossible to pretend that she hadn't seen him. And he would know for sure now that it had been her at the stadium.

Taking a deep breath, Alys put a warning hand under her aunt's elbow before glancing up at him and coming to a stop. Titus, too, stood still. If he had been shocked to see her he had got over it by now and she could read nothing in the quick look she gave him, but there was a grimly sardonic note in his voice as he said, 'Hello, Alys. What a surprise.'

'Yes, isn't it?' Even to Alys's own ears her voice sounded stilted and unnatural. 'Are you—are you on the cruise?'

'Yes. I'm one of the lecturers.'

'Oh. I hadn't realised.'

'No, I was sure you couldn't have done,' Titus said with open irony.

Her eyes swung to meet his then and found in them cool contempt. Trying fiercely to stay calm, Alys tightened her grip on her poor aunt's arm as she pulled her forward. 'I don't think you've met my aunt, Miss Norris. I'm here as her—sort of companion. This is Titus Irvine,' she introduced. 'I—er—met him while I was at college.'

'How do you do?' Aunt Lou shook hands with Titus and managed a smile, but they were blocking the doorway and people wanted to pass, so that they had only time to nod at each other before they had to move out of the way.

She and Alys went into the next room but Alys didn't even bother to look at the famous statue; she kept glancing over her shoulder into the previous room to make sure Titus hadn't turned round to look at her, but he strode straight out of the building.

'Would you please let go of my arm now?' Aunt Lou begged. 'He's gone and you're hurting me.'

'Oh, sorry.' Alys gave her a contrite look. 'I'm treating you rather roughly today, aren't I?'

'It's quite understandable.' She gave Alys an encouraging smile. 'Well, you're over the first and worst hurdle. It wasn't so bad, was it?'

'No,' Alys lied, and gave a mental shudder. She had hoped against hope that Titus would greet her with calm indifference, proving that their relationship had been forgotten. He would never just ignore her, she knew that; Titus had never sulked. But she had never expected such open contempt, such a sign that he, too, hadn't forgotten the past. What chance was there now of her aunt's hope that they could bury their differences? More than ever Alys wanted to run away and hide, but it was too late now; she had no choice but to see it through.

'Do you really want to look at these broken statues?' she demanded tersely.

Aunt Louise gave a small sigh, but said obligingly, 'No, of course not. Do you want to go back to the ship?'

'Yes, please.'

'All right, but I *would* like to buy a guide book and some postcards.'

She made her purchases and they walked out to where the line of coaches were waiting to collect them, the cruise director standing to count the passengers as each bus was filled and left. They were in time to see Gail Turnbull walk up to the coach that Titus was just about to board. He politely stood back for her to get on first and she addressed some laughing remark to him as she did so.

'What has she done with her mother?' Aunt Lou wondered.

'Abandoned her, by the look of it. She's only just coming out of the museum.'

They watched Mrs Gilbert look round for Gail then give a resigned shrug and make her way to the waiting line of passengers. Aunt Lou, followed by Alys, immediately went back to talk to her, making all the usual small talk about the site they'd just visited.

'This is my first visit, but Gail has been here before, of course,' Mrs Gilbert explained by way of excusing her daughter's absence.

The two older women began to chat and Alys let them get in front of her. Titus's coach left and they boarded the next one, Alys insisting that the two ladies stay together while she took the seat behind them. Thankfully no one came to sit next to her and she was able to gaze out of the window, wondering what Titus was thinking now. Her biggest, most agonising fear was that he would think this too much of a coincidence and that she had engineered the whole thing just to see him again. But if she'd wanted to do that there were easier ways of arranging an accidental meeting than going to the length of booking the same cruise. Alys fervently hoped he would reason that way, but Titus was very astute; she couldn't be sure that he hadn't guessed the truth. Maybe that explained the contempt in his eyes. And if he thought that then no amount of argument would make him believe it had all been her aunt's doing, that she hadn't known he was on board until she'd seen him in the stadium.

What would his attitude be towards her once they were back on the ship? Alys wondered. Would he go out of his way to avoid her? She certainly hoped so. And it looked as if Gail had latched on to him, which would make it easier; he could give his attention to the other girl whenever Alys was around. It would be a strange sensation, watching him with another woman, smiling and talking with her, making her feel good, the way he had once been with her. From the moment they had met he had made her feel very special, had never looked at another woman. Alys had believed she was the only woman he had ever wanted, the only person he had ever loved, the girl he had been waiting to meet all his life. She had felt so safe in his love, cocooned by it, uplifted by its purity. And she in turn had loved Titus to the point of adoration and worship. He had been perfect in her eyes, which was probably why it had come as such a tremendous blow when he had finally told her about his past.

And what should her attitude to him be? That was an even bigger worry; she had no control over Titus's behaviour but she did over her own. Well, whatever she did she mustn't make it look as if she *wanted* to see him, talk to him. She must play it very cool, not ignore him of course, but show him that she was completely over him, that he meant nothing to her any more. She must be—indifferent, yes, that was the word. That must be her mantra. And with luck and determination she might live from hour to hour, day to day, and eventually, in what seemed the long-distant future, get through the next two weeks. But whether she would have purged Titus from her heart by then, as her aunt hoped, Alys very much doubted.

When they got back to the ship there was only time to wash before lunch. The ship had two restaurants: the large main one in the centre of the ship, and a smaller taverna type on the upper deck where a buffet was served. Her aunt being a light eater, they went to the latter and joined the queue to select their food. It was strange; yesterday she hadn't seen Titus at all, today she seemed to see him everywhere. He came to stand behind them in the queue and nodded briefly when Alys glanced round and noticed him. She swallowed, not knowing whether to say anything or not, but luckily Aunt Lou came to her rescue by saying, 'Dr Irvine. Hello again. Is this your first tour with the cruise company?'

'Yes. I usually go to Egypt.'

'Oh, a favourite place of mine. I went there with a friend a few years ago and we had the most wonderful time.' Her aunt chatted on about her holiday, Titus politely turning in her direction, but Alys had stopped listening. Aunt Lou had told her to try to remember only the happy times and now, without any effort on her part, they came sweeping back; the first time they had kissed, made love; a never-to-be-forgotten night soon after they had moved into their little house, when a storm raged outside and Titus had quoted love poems to her as he slowly undressed her in the firelight; an afternoon of the most passionate lovemaking in the dappled sunlight of a woodland glade. Memories that she had deliberately tried to suppress because they were too poignant, too unbearably painful. But now they seared into her mind, into the sensual depths of her soul, putting an instant torch to flames that had never completely died away. Shaken by the sudden surge of emotion, Alys gave an unsteady gasp and Titus immediately swung his head round to look at her. Somehow she managed to smother it in a cough, but his eyes stayed on her, alert, probing, searching for the memories that filled her heart. Alys tried desperately to hide them, but perhaps something of them lingered in her wide, vulnerable eyes, because Titus's glance sharpened and he took a half-step towards her, ignoring poor Aunt Lou, whose voice trailed away.

'Ah, Irvine. I don't think you've met my wife.'

They both glanced quickly round as one of the other lecturers came along at that moment, his wife smiling a greeting, and Titus had to turn and shake hands, be polite. The queue moved up, and Alys thankfully picked up a tray, turned her back on Titus and determinedly didn't look in his direction again.

It was so warm that many of the passengers had taken their food outside to eat, sitting on the yellow-mattressed loungers with the trays on their laps. Most people had chosen to sit in the sun but Alys found two together in the shade and settled her aunt there. Titus followed them out on to the deck and glanced round for an empty lounger. There was one next to Alys. She saw him notice it, visibly hesitate, and then turn quickly as he heard his name called and Gail waved to him. 'I've saved you one over here,' she called. Again Titus hesitated, but then made his way over to the other girl.

The lesser of two evils, Alys thought, reading his mind. Poor Titus; how he must wish himself anywhere but here.

'That girl is making herself very obvious,' her aunt remarked reprovingly.

'She's between husbands. She's looking for number three.'

'And does she think a college don would make a nice change?'

Alys smiled, liking her aunt's dry sense of humour. 'Possibly, but I think she's decided to latch on to Titus before anyone else grabs him because he's the only decent-looking single man among the passengers.'

'He's certainly that. I had no idea he was such a handsome man. Only I suppose you think handsome is an old-fashioned word nowadays; what do you say instead—dishy?'

'I think perhaps good-looking or attractive,' Alys suggested, keeping a straight face. Glancing across to where Titus and Gail were sitting, she saw that he was bending towards her, listening as Gail talked animatedly, occasionally touching his arm lightly to make sure she kept his attention. A flash of emotion that was all too familiar suddenly surged through Alys's heart. Oh, God, not that too, she thought miserably. To be jealous just because Titus was sitting with another woman, one he probably didn't even like, was utterly ridiculous, especially after all this time. With wretched insight, Alys realised that her emotions were still raw and primitive where Titus was concerned. Not only the desire that had drawn her to him, but also the jealousy that had torn them apart were still there, both emotions threatening to make her life totally unhappy again.

But at least Alys was adult enough now to recognise the feelings for what they were and try to fight them. She held on to that thought as the ship changed course a little, bringing her chair into the sun. She welcomed the chance to put on her sunglasses so that her aunt couldn't see the despair in her eyes.

But she had been silent for too long and her aunt said, 'Are you all right, my dear?'

'Yes, of course. Fine,' she answered, so brightly that it could only be a lie.

'You never did tell me much about what happened between you and Titus. Would you like to tell me now?'

Alys hesitated; she had told her parents her reason for leaving Titus, told them when she was still full of her first overpowering fury, but their reactions had been so strong that she'd often regretted it. Since then she had been more circumspect, because of her own humiliation and shattered self-confidence as much as anything. Telling anyone about it, even thinking about it, still hurt, so much that she was reluctant to talk about it even now. But perhaps her aunt had a right to know, although she might then feel guilty for having tricked Alys into coming on the trip. And right now those feelings of deep need and jealousy were too strong for her to tell it with any impartiality. So she shook her head and said unsteadily, 'I'm sorry, no. Not here, not now.'

'Of course, my dear. I quite understand. I shouldn't have asked.'

'I think you have the right to ask; I just don't feel able to talk about it at the moment.'

'Then shall we look at the day's programme?' Aunt Louise suggested, accepting her decision and briskly changing the subject. 'There's an illustrated talk on plants of the Mediterranean at three. That's in the lounge. And we shall be entering the Corinth Canal at approximately four-thirty.' She turned over the single sheet of the ship's daily programme. 'And while we go through the canal we're to have a talk on deck by—oh, by Titus, on its history.'

'Really?' Alys managed to keep her voice as calm as her aunt's. 'That isn't his field at all. I bet he's been madly mugging it up in his cabin.'

'Will you come to the lecture on plants?'

'Do you mind if I don't? I think I'd like to go and sunbathe up in the solarium for a while.'

'Of course not. But mind you don't get burnt; the sun is very hot at midday, you know.'

'I'll be careful,' Alys promised and went down to the cabin to change into a swimsuit.

Although she had a fragile look about her, Alys's figure was slim and athletic, almost boyish, from the constant exercise she got in her job, part of which was to teach swimming. At the school she wore a sedate swimsuit but for sunbathing she had treated herself to a strapless one that was cut away high in the legs. It didn't reveal anything but it didn't hide much either. Alys took it out to put on, thought of the possibility of Titus catching sight of her in it, and an immediate tremor of awareness ran through her. Sitting down on the bed, she tried to pull herself together. This is crazy, she thought almost angrily. But it had been such a shock to see Titus again; she could hardly be expected to get over it in just a few hours. It would take time. Time that she'd promised both Aunt Lou and herself wouldn't be spent moping in the cabin, so she had better do as she'd intended and go and sunbathe, Alys thought determinedly. Putting on the swimsuit, with a towelling robe over it, she made her way back to the upper deck, carefully not looking towards where Titus and Gail had been sitting, and to the stairs leading up to the tiny sundeck above the pool bar.

There were a couple of elderly people there, soaking up the sun, their skin already deeply tanned. Alys could imagine them sitting in deckchairs in their garden every day, enjoying their retirement. They took no notice of her as she settled herself in a corner and took out the book she'd brought to read. Her own arms and legs were already a pale gold from playing tennis, but her shoulders were whiter than her limbs. Not like Gail, she thought, who had a beautifully even tan.

Just before three the couple roused themselves and went down to the lounge for the lecture on plants. Alys tried to concentrate on her book. Thinking that she'd have lots of time on her hands, she'd treated herself to several of what she called 'pleasure' books, mostly novels by authors she hadn't tried before. She'd been looking forward to reading them, but that was before she'd found out that Titus was on board. Now she found it almost impossible to lose herself in the book as she normally did. Instead she sat back and closed her eyes, but then she kept remembering past incidents with Titus, both good and bad—but somehow her errant mind now kept remembering mostly the bad. Then she would determinedly chase them away and try to keep her mind on something else, but always her thoughts found their way back to Titus.

Angry with herself, Alys got quickly to her feet, dropped her sunglasses on the lounger, ran down the stairs and jumped into the empty pool. It was only a few yards wide, useless for burning off inner anger and frustration, but she did her best, diving to the bottom and up again, and counting the number of continuous somersaults she could do until she had to stop and rest. Slowly now, she climbed the steps from the pool and stood on the wooden deck, immediately assailed by the heat. Reaching up, she pushed her hair back and wrung the water out of it with her hands, her face tilted towards the sky, eyes closed, her figure, outlined in the wet swimsuit, young and intimately feminine.

Perhaps it was some instinct that warned her that she was being watched. Looking towards the pool bar she saw the young Greek barman, a rapt smile on his face, and sitting on one of the stools an older man, perhaps in his early forties, with an equally appreciative look in his eyes. Thinking that she had found her watchers, Alys turned away—and was devastated to find that Titus was still there.

He was alone now, though, and had changed into a pair of shorts, his shirt cast aside. All the other passengers had gone to the lecture and she hadn't noticed him when she'd run so quickly across the deck, and it had been impossible to see him from the pool. But did he know that? Did he think that she was flaunting herself for his sake?

His eyes were on her, quite openly watching, and her first instinct was to cover herself—which was completely irrational when she'd lived with the man for over two years. There was nothing of her body that he didn't know, nowhere that he hadn't caressed and kissed, and delighted in the doing—running his hands over her, exploring, creating that passionate, aching need that only he could assuage.

Her thoughts must have shown in her face, in the tenseness of her body. Titus lowered the book he was holding and sat up straight on the lounger. Quickly, ashamed of her thoughts, Alys looked round for her robe, but she'd left it on the upper deck, and she hadn't thought to bring a towel. But the man who'd been sitting at the bar strode forward and handed one to her.

'Need this?'

'Oh. Yes. Thanks.'

'You looked to be working off a lot of energy in there,' the man remarked as she began to towel herself dry, her back to Titus.

'Did I?' She laughed nervously, not really taking any notice of the man, her senses still in chaos.

'Have you been sunbathing? You must be careful, you know. I don't want to have to treat you for sunstroke.'

'Treat me?' She blinked and tried to concentrate. 'Oh, I see; you're the ship's doctor.'

'That's right. Jack Reed. You look rather flushed. Come and have a drink and cool down.'

Alys hesitated, very much aware of Titus listening and watching, but then she thought, To hell with him, and her chin came up as she nodded. 'Thanks, that would be nice.'

They sat on the bar stools and Alys watched as the Greek barman mixed long drinks for them, making a showy performance out of it because he had her attention.

'This your first cruise with the touring company?' the doctor asked.

'Yes—although I didn't actually choose the holiday; my aunt's friend couldn't come at the last minute so I took her place.' She didn't know whether Titus was listening or not, or even if he could hear from where he was sitting, but she said it clearly, hoping he could.

'I'm not surprised; they don't get many young unattached girls on these trips, Miss...?'

'Oh, sorry. Alys Curtis. And, yes, it is Miss.' She took a sip of her drink. 'And are you with the ship permanently?'

He laughed and shook his head. 'No, just for this trip.' Leaning forward, he said in a lowered voice, 'You get the cruise free in return for your services. Just like the lecturers.'

'Oh, I see.' Alys smiled at him, thinking that he must be an overworked hospital doctor, or perhaps out of work altogether. 'Would you like to stay on longer?'

'Wouldn't mind. The sun and sea are just what I need. Only drawback is I have to accompany all the excursions in case someone takes ill. Must say, though, that all the pensioners are a fit lot; most of them left me panting behind at Delphi.'

The mention of Delphi brought back too sharp a memory; Alys looked down at her drink, longing to glance at Titus to see if he was listening, but afraid of betraying herself if she did. But maybe he had heard because he sauntered over and sat on a stool at the other end of the bar, ordered a drink.

'Have this on me,' Jack Reed offered.

'I don't want to intrude on you and your—friend,' Titus returned smoothly, but with a sardonic edge that only Alys detected.

His tone made Alys's chin come up and her eyes harden. Good; his coolness helped to still the inner panic that his closeness and the sight of his bare, broad chest had brought.

'The more the merrier,' Jack said expansively. It appeared that he and Titus had already met at a briefing for the doctor and lecturers, but he introduced Alys. She nodded without speaking, refusing to acknowledge that they already knew each other unless Titus did. But he merely gave her a coolly mocking look and said, 'Enjoy your swim?'

'Not really; the pool was too small.'

'It didn't seem to cramp your style.'

Alys frowned, then realised that it was a *double entendre* and that he was really referring to her having a drink with Jack. Her hand tightened on her glass. 'Have you dipped into the pool yet?'

'Not yet.'

'Really? I quite thought you had.' And she gave him an overly innocent smile.

Titus knew full well that she was obliquely alluding to Gail. He gave a lazy grin. 'I'm afraid the pool is too small for me,' he answered. 'I prefer something bigger.'

'Like the sea? Be careful you don't get caught by an octopus.'

'Knowing what they're like, I'm quite sure I'd be able to avoid the tentacles if I saw another.'

Jack glanced from one to the other of them, perhaps sensing the strong undercurrent of tension. 'I don't think the fish in the Med are big enough to do you any harm.'

'No,' Alys agreed. 'It's probably the other way round.'

Titus smiled thinly, but it seemed he was content to leave their war of hidden words because he started talking to Jack about the speed and history of the ship.

It had been very quiet on the deck, but suddenly there was a burst of noise and the passengers, the lecture over, came pouring out to find good places for their journey through the Corinth Canal. People came to the bar, getting between them, so that it was now impossible to talk. Titus swallowed down his beer, thanked Jack, gave Alys a derisive nod, and went through the doors into the ship. Alys chatted to the doctor as naturally as she could after a run-in with a man who excited both need and anger in about equal parts, until she'd finished her drink, then excused herself and went up to the sundeck to collect her things, before going back down to the cabin to shower and change.

It seemed that the person giving the deck lecture didn't actually stand among the passengers but up on the bridge where he could use the ship's loud-speaker system. Alys stood on the shadowed side of the deck, where there were few people, while she listened. And although she heard him telling how ships had originally been dragged by hand across the Isthmus, it was Titus's voice that held her. He had a deep, well-modulated voice, exactly right for holding an audience when he gave a lecture. He also had the ability to imbue his listeners with his own enthusiasm and love for his subject, a talent that had made him an excellent tutor. Alys had heard it often when he had been a lecturer at university. Although Egyptology wasn't Alys's field she had gone along and quickly become converted, changing courses in mid-stream, foreseeing the shared interest lasting a lifetime. They would go together on digs, she would be his assistant, his secretary, his sounding-board. So long as she and Titus were together she didn't much care what she did.

And she had heard his voice, too, when it was husky with desire, thick with passion, when it whispered the most wonderful compliments, and when it had cried out her name at the height of sexual excitement. And she had heard it when he had said fervently, 'I love you, Alys. Love you, love you, love you.'

If you say it thrice it must be true, she thought, but then silly tears came into her eyes. She blinked them away, staring unseeingly up at the sheer sides of the canal, towering above the ship and only a few feet away. 'Try to remember only the happy times', her aunt had said, but the happy times made her even more sad than the bad.

Alys leaned against the rail, gripping it tightly. Too many memories were coming back, too many old emotions stirred. She had walked out on Titus but she hadn't stopped loving him. And she knew now that she never would. But learn to live with it? Every moment that she heard his voice only made that seem more impossible.

CHAPTER THREE

AFTER the lecture everyone had to go to their stations for lifeboat drill, Alys and Aunt Louise finding themselves in the same group as Gail and her mother.

'Oh, dear,' Louise murmured to Alys. 'I hate to be uncharitable, but I do hope we don't have to abandon ship and spend ages in a boat with them. Mrs Gilbert has become rather confiding—I'm already on to Gail's second marriage.'

'We'll try to avoid them in future, then,' Alys promised with a grin, supremely confident that Louise would never confide *her* problems to any chance acquaintance.

Tonight was the captain's cocktail party followed by a gala dinner. Alys was tempted to dress down, to put on a simple cotton dress and merge with all the middle-aged passengers. But then she remembered Titus; she didn't want him to think she'd become a complete frump, did she? Pride said certainly not, so Alys put on one of her glitzy numbers: a simple black sheath dress with a shortish skirt, but with a richly beaded black jacket to go over it. With black tights and high heels, her blonde hair left long and straight, Alys knew she looked good. Rather sophisticated and remote, but good. Just the way she wanted to be when Titus was around.

Gail had chosen to wear red, obviously one of her favourite colours. Her mother trailed behind her in the receiving line like a flustered brown hen, but wasn't altogether displeased when the captain, a dapper little man, gave Gail a lot of attention. He gave Alys an appreciative once-over, too, but she responded with her most glacial smile and moved to follow her aunt, who had determinedly become blind as she walked past Gail and her mother to join another group. Drinks were served, people circulated. There were a few more of the ship's officers there, and they talked to one of the lecturers and his wife, he a clergyman, she dressed like a Sixties flower-child in long, full skirt and open sandals—a woman who must have been about fifty but determined not to grow up, let alone to age gracefully.

There were several clichéd characters there, Alys thought with amusement, looking round. An earth mother, very big and bosomy, an ex-army major with loud voice and moustache, three stick-thin American sisters, all with fluffy blonde hair, who looked as if they ought once to have been a singing trio—and probably were. And then there was Titus. Partly hidden by the earth mother, Alys watched as he shook hands with the captain. He was wearing evening clothes, as all the men were, but he had a white tuxedo and red bow-tie rather than the usual black suit. He looked—just terrific. And the sight of him started a fierce ache deep inside her that physically hurt.

Wrenching her eyes away, Alys began to mutter, 'I'm indifferent, indifferent, indifferent,' under her breath.

'Good enough to eat, isn't he?'

Startled, she turned to see that Gail had come up beside her.

'I saw you looking at our divine Dr Irvine.' She put a hand on Alys's arm. 'And to think I didn't want to come on this trip. I had no idea intellectuals could be so gorgeous. Are all schoolmasters like that nowadays?'

'Not quite.'

'No, I didn't think they were. Excuse me.'

She went to move away, to intercept Titus, Alys strongly suspected, but just then Jack Reed came up to them.

'Hello, Miss Curtis, or may I call you Alys?'

'Of course. This is Mrs Turnbull,' Alys said quickly before Gail could get away. 'Have you met Jack Reed, the ship's doctor?'

'No, I haven't.' She was sufficiently vain to want every man to admire her, so Gail gave him a warm smile as she shook his hand.

Jack blinked a little but responded with a big grin. 'If anyone's going to trip and sprain their ankle on this trip I do hope it will be one of you two girls—it will make the whole voyage worthwhile.'

Gail laughed delightedly, making people turn to look at her, and Alys smiled, thinking that Jack was a bit of a flirt. He looked as good as he ever would, she thought, in a black evening suit that was well cut but still managed to look casual on him. But perhaps his easygoing air was too casual, perhaps it was a mask for something. Gail was talking to him, making him laugh, but her eyes constantly flicked across the room to where Titus stood with a couple of lecturers and their wives. A few of the passengers were wearing the name-tags that had been supplied with their tickets, but most of them, including the lecturers, hadn't bothered.

The cruise director came round, breaking up groups, making people circulate. Gail took the opportunity to go over to Titus, but she didn't draw him away, as Alys expected, instead getting him to introduce her to the people with him and then stand by his side as if they were a couple. Clever tactics, Alys realised. She and her aunt had moved on but Jack Reed ambled with them, which she wasn't too happy about. She didn't want to have Jack or anyone else attach himself to her—for her own sake, her aunt's, and mostly because she didn't want Titus to think that she was on the lookout for a man and deliberately encouraging him.

Whether it was her doing or Titus's, they managed to avoid each other during the party, and she was amused to see that he also managed to avoid sitting with Gail during dinner. The two walked into the restaurant together, but after he had seated Gail and her mother he gallantly gave up his place to a lone, lost-looking elderly lady. Alys almost laughed aloud at the look of chagrin that flashed in Gail's eyes. But watching Titus and Gail had made her own attention slip and she found herself on the same table as Jack Reed, although she did manage to put Aunt Lou between them.

The restaurant had been decorated with flowers and the waiters wore traditional Greek dress. There was Greek food and plenty of wine. Everyone was very jolly and really getting into the swing of the holiday. People were speaking to each other on first-name terms now and tended to stay in their groups when they went up to the lounge for coffee after dinner. Several, however, went out on deck to watch as the ship berthed at the little island of Hydra, Alys's group among them. It was already dark, but as the ship nosed into the horseshoe-shaped bay they saw the lights of the port and the town above it spread like a glistening tiara against the sky.

'Oh, how lovely!' Aunt Louise exclaimed. 'We must go ashore for a while.'

The dock wasn't long enough for the ship and they had to anchor close to a long concrete mole and dis-embark through the door in the ship's side that the crew normally used, a sailor standing at the awkward gang-plank to help the less able-bodied ashore. Houses climbed the steep hills leading from the waterfront and there were little cobbled alleys that zigzagged between them, lit by occasional streetlights attached to the walls. The night air was very still and heavy with a spicy, musky scent, the warmth of the land coming out to meet them.

They walked slowly along, about seven of them in their group, and took a leisurely stroll, glancing in the windows of jewellery and souvenir shops, avoiding dogs and cats, and promenading dark-eyed islanders. The two other couples decided to buy hats for themselves and went into a shop, but the doctor stayed with Alys and Aunt Lou as they walked on. In the inner harbour there were several luxury yachts, their occupants eating or sitting over a drink at one of the pavement cafés. Music came from the open window of a bar up the hill: Greek music, lively, insinuating. The waterfront wasn't very long, less than half a mile, but it was enough for Aunt Louise. 'It's been a long day,' she declared, 'what with Delphi this morning. I think I'll make my way back to the ship. But you don't have to come, my dear; I can manage quite well alone.'

'I think I would like to stay a bit longer.' Alys turned to Jack Reed. 'Perhaps you'd be kind enough to escort my aunt back to the ship?'

'Of course.' But he came up to her and lowered his voice to ask, 'May I come back and join you or am I being dismissed?'

'I'd like to be alone for a while, if you don't mind. It seems an awfully long time since I was alone.' But Alys smiled to show that there was no animosity in her words.

He nodded. 'Goodnight, then.' And strode after her aunt.

Alys walked slowly to a nearby café which had little palm trees in tubs among the tables. She sat at one in a chair facing the sea, her back determinedly turned against a tank where a couple of small octopuses swam, waiting to be chosen and eaten. She ordered a drink and, feeling very European, watched the people strolling along, both visitors and native islanders. Several passengers from the ship went by, some of whom greeted her. Then she saw Titus. He was with a group of people, Gail among them—which was no surprise. Alys felt her chest grow tight, realising that she would have to acknowledge them, but the waiter came with her drink as they passed, so she merely gave the group a general nod before turning away.

They went past, came to the end of the waterfront and turned to retrace their footsteps. Alys was able to ignore them by lifting her glass to her mouth this time, but nearly choked when she heard Titus say, 'Excuse me. Someone I know. Goodnight.' And he abruptly left the others to walk over to her table. Gail made a surprised gesture of protest, but there was nothing she could do, and after a moment she moved on with the rest.

Alys coughed a couple of times, trying to recover.

'Are you all right?' Titus stood with his hands on the back of a chair, waiting for her either to invite him to sit down or tell him to go and drown himself in the harbour, presumably.

'Yes, fine. A lemon pip went down the wrong way.'

'I think we ought to talk, don't you?'

There was nothing at all conciliatory in his tone, which made it easier for her to say coldly, 'If you insist.'

Titus sat down, flicked his finger at the waiter and ordered a drink. They were silent until it came, Alys very aware of the sound of the water lapping against the harbour wall, of the click-clack of heels on the stone pavement, worn smooth and shiny by countless feet. She tried very hard not to think of other times when they had sat together at cafés like this, when there had been love and contentment between them instead of this taut, wary hostility.

The waiter set his drink before him and Titus picked it up, stirring it with a circular motion of his hand. 'This is quite a coincidence,' he remarked.

'Isn't it?' she replied unhelpfully.

'I took the place of a lecturer who couldn't come at the last minute.'

'So I heard.' She wondered why he found it necessary to explain.

He fell silent again, then lifted his glass and took a long swallow, as if he was very thirsty. 'How are you?' The question was jerked out as if he was reluctant to ask.

'I'm fine,' she answered unsteadily. 'And you?'

He shrugged. 'Very well.'

She had to ask it, it was unavoidable, but Alys's mouth was completely dry as she said, 'And your son—I hope he's OK?'

His eyes seared into hers, looking for malice or sarcasm. Finding none, he said shortly, 'He's well enough.'

There were lots more questions she longed to ask but knew it was impossible, so she asked a safe one instead. 'Ancient Greece isn't your line, is it?'

He sat back a little, tilting the chair. 'I've widened my scope since—during the last couple of years.'

Since she'd left him, had he been going to say? Had he taken on the extra study to try and fill the long, empty hours of loneliness? But he had had his son—and his son's mother. While she'd had—nothing, nothing at all.

She didn't speak, couldn't, but after a long, uncomfortable moment Titus said, 'Did you take your doctorate?'

Putting a hand under the table, Alys dug her nails into her fist, the pain somehow helping her to shake her head and say, 'No. I left university straight—straight away.'

He was watching her but she didn't meet his eyes. 'That's what I heard. That was——' he searched for the right words, tactful words, she realised '—a great pity, a great waste. I'm sorry.'

Her head came up at that. 'Why the hell should you be sorry? It was my decision. If anything I'd been wasting my time taking the course in Egyptology in the first place.'

Titus's jaw hardened. 'Just as you'd wasted your time being with me, I suppose?'

'As it worked out, yes,' Alys retorted, her cheeks flushed. But then she bit her lip and slowly shook her head. 'No, that's not true. I don't—regret it.'

His left eyebrow rose. 'You would appear to have grown up a little.'

'Don't be so damn patronising!'

A flash of amusement came into Titus's eyes but was quickly gone. 'So what are you doing now?'

'I'm a teacher—at a quite good girls' school.' This last was added defensively as she looked for derision in his face. She was right; he laughed.

'So you ran to hide yourself in the modern equivalent of a nunnery, did you? I might have guessed.'

She glared at him. 'And just what is that supposed to mean?'

'You know full well what I mean; life became real instead of the beautiful dream you expected it to be and you couldn't handle it. So, like the coward you are, you turned and ran rather than face up to it. Just the way you ran when you saw me at Delphi this morning.'

'Don't you dare call me a coward!'

Titus gave a mocking laugh. 'I was wrong; you haven't changed at all.'

Alys was about to make a crushing retort, but suddenly realised that they were already fighting again. Biting her lip, she sat back in her chair, then said shakily, 'It seems that neither of us has.'

They were silent, both remembering the past, then Titus finished his drink and set the glass down on the table with a snap. 'Would you like another drink?'

'No, thank you,' Alys replied, adding stiffly, 'Don't let me keep you. Gail will have got back to the ship by now—you should be safe so long as she isn't waiting to grab you when you go on board.'

He grinned suddenly and it tore her heart. 'I'm hoping she'll take the hint.'

'Well, I'm glad I came in handy.'

'And I see you managed to ditch the doctor. Was that because you don't fancy him—or simply because he's a man?'

'I have nothing against men in general.'

'Only me in particular, I suppose.'

She shrugged and he gave a contemptuous laugh but didn't pursue it, instead signalling the waiter for more drinks, ignoring her refusal.

'Why did you run away from me this morning?' Titus asked curtly in a tone she recognised, one that demanded an answer.

She thought about it before saying carefully, 'Delphi is a magical kind of place. To be alone in that stadium with so many ghosts... I closed my eyes to try to get closer to them. When I opened them I was dazzled by the sun—and then you walked out of the shadows.'

'You thought I was a ghost?'

'More a figment of my imagination. For a minute or two. I couldn't believe that it was really you. I expected you to dissolve or something. But then Gail came.'

'And you ran.'

'I needed time to recover, I admit that.'

'Yes, I suppose you might.' But his expression hadn't softened any.

Their drinks came and while he was paying the waiter Alys was able to study him more closely. The lines around his mouth had deepened, but whether that was because of her she didn't know. Otherwise there was nothing different about him; his hair was as thick and dark as ever, his body just as toned and supple. He must still do the course of exercises that she had taught him, the work-out that they'd done together every morning—unless of course they'd made love when they'd woken; then they'd been too exhausted for anything energetic afterwards.

The waiter went away, pleased with his tip, and Titus turned back to her.

'How long have we got?' she asked quickly.

'Till midnight.'

She smiled slightly. 'Like Cinderella.'

'That's right; when the church clock strikes the hour the ship will change into a tramp steamer.'

'And the crew into fish.'

'The slipper into a sea boot.'

'Aunt Louise into Neptune.'

'And Gail into a shark,' Titus finished with feeling.

They looked at each other and suddenly burst into laughter. But both quickly sobered, Alys feeling a great sense of loss. 'A touch of *déjà vu*,' she said unsteadily.

'It wasn't all bad,' Titus said on a curt note.

'No.' Alys looked across at him, her eyes tender with remembered love. 'Most of it was—magnificent.' She said the word on a long sigh, but then blinked and looked down at her glass, letting her hair fall forward to hide the sudden tears that came into her eyes.

Titus didn't speak, and after a moment she raised her head, pushed her hair back with her hand, and took a long drink. They watched in silence as a small boat, its engine noisy, came into the harbour and pulled up beside the steps in a practised, efficient movement. It was brightly painted and had an orange light at the mast. It dropped its passengers, they paid, and the sea taxi was away again, back to the mainland.

When it had gone the silence suddenly became heavy, unbearable. 'What did you think of Delphi?' Alys asked in a determinedly casual tone.

'I think I've heard that question about thirty times today.'

She was immediately annoyed. 'I'm sorry to be so mundane.'

'Don't get prickly.'

'You should have stayed with Gail, then; I'm quite sure she would have been absolutely charming.'

'Maybe I should.'

'Only she isn't your type, is she?'

His jaw thrusting forward, Titus said brusquely, 'No. And we both know what my type is, don't we?'

For a moment her heart fluttered crazily and she could only stare at him, taken aback by his openness. But then Alys managed to pull herself together a little and say carefully, 'I know what it *was*. You might have—altered your view since then.'

'So I might,' he concurred harshly. 'You certainly gave me reason enough.'

It was a good job that her glass was a serviceable one, thick and tough, otherwise it would probably have broken as Alys's hand tightened on it suddenly, her knuckles showing white. Taking refuge in anger she said acidly, 'Do we have to talk about the past? As far as I'm concerned it's dead and done with.'

'"Dead and done with".' Titus repeated the phrase, his eyes bleak for a moment as he looked at her, but then they grew contemptuous again as he said, 'And yet you ran away today.'

She stood up, really angry now. 'But not far enough, unfortunately.'

'So what are you going to do—leave the ship? Run away again?'

It was an idea that was becoming infinitely more attractive by the minute. But there had been a sneer in his tone that put her back up, and, besides, he had already accused her of cowardice. So Alys's head came up and she said icily, 'Sorry to disappoint you, but I really don't see why I should have my holiday ruined by something as—as trivial as this. So if you don't like me being here, then I suggest that *you* leave.'

Titus gave a short, derisive laugh. '*I* don't run away from my commitments.'

Alys looked at him for a long moment, knowing that to go on with this conversation would only make things worse. Picking up her bag, she swung it on her shoulder. 'Thanks for the drink, Titus—it was some reunion.' And she turned to stride back along the waterfront.

He didn't follow immediately but then she heard his step some way behind her, a step she had learnt and listened for so often when they were together, running to meet him, longing to be held close to him again after even the shortest absences. Now her stride lengthened in her hurry to get away.

Two young men, obviously Greeks, were in her path. Alys went to move round them but they moved in the same direction, bringing her to a halt. 'You drink with me and him?' The English was terrible but it hardly mattered—the eyes that coveted her body and the hand that reached out to touch her hair said it all. She jerked away, her hair a live halo, swirling around her head. Titus's step quickened and he came up to them. He put a hand on her shoulder and made a very primitive gesture with the other. Possession and threat. The two young Greeks looked at the purpose in his face and the strength in his shoulders and melted away into the night.

Alys didn't thank him, didn't even look at him, just moved out of his hold and continued on towards the ship. But this time Titus kept pace with her so that they were together as they walked along the mole where the ship was moored, a great many of the passengers still on the deck. And it was his hand that went under her elbow to help her on to the gangplank.

But once on board Alys made her way to the nearest ladies' room and stayed there for some time, bathing her hot temples and her wrists, trying to still her raging thoughts, trying to stop her hands shaking. The ship's siren sounded to warn the last passengers that they were about to sail. Alys took a long look at herself in the mirror, wondering how the hell she was going to survive this trip. Two women came in, friends, chattering and laughing. Drying her hands, Alys left the cloakroom and

went out on to the deck. Most of the passengers were
out there, in the bow, watching as the ship prepared to
sail, but Alys turned and went to the steps leading up
to the sundeck.

It was empty; the elderly didn't climb steep stairs unless
they had to. Leaning against the rail, Alys watched as
the ship backed slowly out of the harbour, unable to
turn in the narrow confines. The lights on the waterfront gradually diminished, the spicy scent of the land
giving way to the saltiness of the sea. They had invaded
the intensely insular life of the island for a few hours,
been welcomed for the money they might spend, and
were already forever forgotten. Just another ship. Just
another load of tourists. But Alys thought that she would
never forget the little island that had emerged out of the
darkness and that was now melting back into it again.
The ship gave one last, farewell blast on the siren, then
turned in a great arc and sailed on, only the waves of
its wake rippling back towards the shore.

Alys stirred, having come to a decision of her own.
When she had left Titus it had been on a tide of intense
emotion. She hadn't thought about it, just acted impulsively—— No, not just on impulse; she had felt driven
to go. It had all seemed so unfair, so terribly unfair. And
after she'd left everything had been too raw and hurting
to dwell on, to go back over time and time again—one
moment to think that it had all been her fault, the next
to be sure that the ménage à trois that Titus wanted was
intolerable. So she had tried to push it all out of her
mind, afraid that—— Her thoughts came to a dizzying
halt. Afraid. Titus had called her a coward—and so had
her aunt. Maybe they were right. It was true that she
had never really faced up to her feelings after she'd left,
never gone back over the events that had led to her des-

perate decision to leave him. But maybe now was the time. If she was to find the courage to go on with this charade of a holiday, then maybe she had first better find the courage to go back and be sure that she had been right to leave the man she loved so much.

Feeling suddenly chill, Alys went quickly down to the cabin. Aunt Lou was sitting up in bed, reading. With a muttered apology, Alys hurried to use the bathroom and change into pyjamas. She climbed into bed and glanced across at the older woman. 'Do we have to get up early tomorrow?'

'No, we have the morning at sea, and the first lecture isn't until nine. So we'll set the alarm for seven forty-five, shall we?'

'That sounds fine.'

Aunt Lou picked up the alarm clock. 'Did you buy anything in Hydra after I left?'

'No, I had a drink in a café.'

'That must have been pleasant.'

'Not really. Titus came along.'

Looking over her glasses, Aunt Lou said, 'Oh. I see.' She turned off the light. 'Goodnight, my dear.'

'Goodnight.'

Alys lay in the darkness, listening to the faintly comforting sounds of the ship's engines, a monotonous noise that last night had sent her to sleep. But tonight she didn't want to sleep. She tried to force her mind back to the years she'd been with Titus, but it kept shying away. Afraid, always afraid. There was only one way, she realised, and said softly into the darkness, 'Aunt Lou, are you asleep?'

'No.' Her aunt immediately understood. 'Only tell me if you're sure you want to.'

Alys sighed deeply. 'I wanted to forget, not try to remember. But now...' She was silent for a moment, trying to conquer her fears.

Reaching out, Aunt Lou took her hand in hers, warm and reassuring. 'I'm listening, my dear.'

CHAPTER FOUR

IT HAD begun with such golden brilliance, like some dazzlingly bright miracle, filling Alys's eyes with radiant happiness, her heart with love. She had been blindingly happy, unable to see anything but the fulfilment of her dreams. But even though they'd both known from the first moment that they were meant for each other, they hadn't rushed things. The opposite almost. They'd known they had all the time in the world, and wanted to savour every moment.

After their meeting on the ferry the two groups had joined and they'd eventually spent the rest of the Easter holiday together on the fells of the Lake District. Sometimes they'd all walked on the lower slopes, on the other days the men had given the girls climbing lessons, and once, at Titus's suggestion, they had all split up and done their own thing.

Alys especially remembered that day. It was the first time that Titus really kissed her. Alone at last, they walked from the hostel where they were staying up into the hills. It was a beautiful day, warm and sunny, the sky a cloudless blue. Birds wheeled and called, their wings translucent in the sunlight. The fields were purple with heather that gave off a heady scent as they brushed it with their feet. They came to the crest of a hill and tacitly stopped, awestruck by the beauty of the view.

Alys let her eyes pan slowly over the scene before her, registering each detail, like a camera, wanting to hold it in her mind forever.

'What are you thinking?' Titus murmured beside her, his arm going round her waist.

'That I want to remember this view, this moment, always.'

He smiled. 'Then I'd better give you something to remember it by.'

Titus drew her slowly to him, his eyes holding hers, darkening with desire. She was already trembling with anticipation even before he lowered his head to find her lips, touching them gently, with exquisite tenderness, like a mortal allowed to sip the nectar of the gods. For quite a while they were content just to touch, to gently explore the other's mouth with tiny, almost tentative kisses, but then Titus ran the tip of his tongue against her lips, probed a little so that Alys slowly opened her mouth to him, like a flower opening its petals. A great tremor of desire ran through him and Titus held her closer against him. His awakening need lit a torch deep inside her own body and Alys moved her hips against his in yearning arousal, a movement as primitive and old as time.

Suddenly everything changed. Titus gave a gasping groan and his hand went low on her hips, holding her tight against him so that she was in no doubt of how much he wanted her. His lips became opportune, demanding and getting the response he sought.

'Titus. Titus.' She moaned his name against his lips as the world began to spin and she was lost to everything but the need to satisfy this terrible, greedy need to be held and kissed and loved. The torch of desire burst into a burning hunger that consumed her whole body, into a flame of passion that would never die.

His fingers gripped her so tightly that they bruised her skin, but she didn't feel it; her hands were on his head, in his hair, holding his mouth against her own, drowning in his kisses. But then Titus broke away, holding her by the length of his arms, his hands gripping her shoulders. His breath was uneven, panting, his mouth parted, and she could feel the wild beating of his heart. But it was his eyes that held her. They were so full of triumphant happiness, like a man who had found his long-sought-for grail and claimed it for his own. Suddenly he dropped his hands to her waist and lifted her high off the ground, then swung her round in giddy circles. 'I love you!' he shouted. 'I love you, Alys.'

And the hills that surrounded them took up his cry, echoing one off another, until the air was full of its mad peal. And for miles around they heard his avowal. 'I love you. I love you, Alys.'

She cried a little then, from happiness, and he kissed her tears away. 'I don't deserve this.'

But Titus laughed at her. 'You deserve everything you're going to get.' A suggestive remark that made her blush crimson and showed her up for the inexperienced girl that she was, but also filled her with an even greater excitement and anticipation.

She thought that Titus might take her there and then, in those heather-clad hills, but it was several weeks before they eventually made love. And he made that perfect, too, taking her with him in the summer to his beloved Egypt, to a small house far from the nearest town. There was a fountain in the courtyard, its tinkling music the accompaniment to that first long night of love. A perfect night. A perfect week, in which they were completely alone and Alys found that it was impossible to be satiated by love. She wanted to be not only close to Titus, but a part of him. She found that he was far more experienced than she, but that he delighted in teaching her, in arousing her to the heights of awareness, and in guiding her so that he, too, was lifted to the groaning peak of excitement and passion.

But there were interludes when they were content just to be together, to be close enough to see, to touch, to hear. After that first week, Titus had to work, and he took her with him to the dig whose progress he had come to report on, taking her into dark and hushed tombs, reading the hieroglyphics on the walls by the light of his torch, showing her the artefacts they'd found, his arm lightly but possessively round her waist as he talked. Then perhaps they would join his colleagues, both British and Egyptian, at a restaurant for dinner, watch the belly-dancers with their whirling skirts, and hold hands under the table, knowing that in a few hours they would be in each other's arms again, each worshipping the other's body with their own.

And there were moments that were forever scorched into her memory, such as when the shower failed and Titus washed her with his bare hands, both of them un-clothed, kissing her as he did so, his eyes ever darkening, until neither of them were able to stand it any longer and he pulled her down on to his lap.

When they went back to England Alys switched to a course on Egyptology at his university and they found a small Edwardian house, moving in together. Alys had thought he would find a flat, because despite being a college lecturer he didn't seem to have a great deal of money, but Titus said he didn't want any neighbours around because he intended to make love to her in every room. She laughed at him and fell ever deeper in love, aware of the contentment and supreme self-confidence that happiness had given him. He seemed somehow to have gained in stature, both mentally and physically, standing proud before the world.

They didn't actually speak of marriage. It was unnecessary really; they both knew that in the fullness of time they would marry and have children. But there was plenty of time, oceans of time. Alys had to get her degree and then work for a doctorate. Titus had papers to write, digs to go on, endless opportunities for advancement. But the first Christmas they were together he gave her a ring, made from an ancient Egyptian scarab, and put it on the third finger of her left hand.

'My love for the past and my love for the future,' he said softly.

They were alone in their house, sitting on the floor in front of the fire, its dancing light the only illumination in the room, a place where they had often made love. 'Oh, Titus, I love you so much,' Alys sighed. Reaching up, she put her hands on either side of his face to kiss him, but a swirl of wind came down the chimney, sending the flames spitting and flaring, and she felt a great sense of dread and desolation, made all the worse by its suddenness. With a whimper of fear Alys flung her arms round him, hugging him to her. 'Don't ever leave me, Titus. Swear you'll never leave me.'

He began to laugh, but then, seeing her terror, he put his arms round her in a great bear-hug, reassuring her with his closeness as well as words. 'You know I'll never leave you. I love you more than life.' And gradually her fears dimmed and she let him make her laugh, but she always remembered that first portent of dread.

For those first two years they were ecstatically happy. Alys got her degree and, that milestone in her life achieved, began to think of her future. She would take her doctorate, of course, but now her thoughts began to turn towards marriage. It was obvious that her parents, who had met and liked Titus, wanted them to legalise their relationship. Not that they said anything; it was their ever-tactful avoidance of the subject that made their feelings clear. Whenever they went to stay at her home, her mother gave them separate rooms, which always added spice to their relationship, because they were both as frustrated as hell.

'If I don't get you into bed soon I shall go blind,' Titus had whispered urgently into her ear once, making Alys burst out laughing.

She smiled, remembering it later, and realised she was ready for marriage. She liked the idea of being openly acknowledged as Titus's wife, instead of his girlfriend. She liked the idea of being called Mrs Irvine, with all that it implied. And she liked the idea of committing herself to Titus forever, and wanted the world to see that he had committed himself to her.

There was another factor, too, that had led her thoughts towards marriage. Theirs hadn't been the only romance that had grown out of the meeting on the ferry. Two of their friends had fallen for each other and had got married in a rush when the man had been offered a post in Australia. Now they wrote that they were expecting their first child. The feeling of envy that this news aroused startled Alys. I must be getting broody, she thought. And why not? She was nearly twenty-three years old and in love for keeps. They could get married and if a baby came along she could still study for her doctorate. Lots of other women did. In her imagination she could see them setting off for a dig somewhere, the child slung in a carrier on Titus's back.

She made tentative noises about marriage and, if anything, Titus seemed pleased. But there was, as always, no great rush. Spring would be nice, she thought, and she wanted a big wedding, one where she could show off Titus to all her friends and relations. She was so proud of him, so in love. But when she got home from college one evening she found a note from Titus saying that he'd had to go away for a couple of days; he didn't know when he would be back. And he left no telephone number or address where he could be contacted. So she waited at home in growing anxiety and bewilderment; he had never done anything like this before. He rang on the first evening, but just said that he'd had to go and see an old college friend. He sounded strained and was unforthcoming, avoiding her questions, so that she became curious and a little annoyed.

The following two days, before he returned, seemed agonisingly long; they had never been apart for so long since they'd started living together. Titus rang again, but still wouldn't tell her what it was all about, which made her angry. In Alys's view, if you loved someone then you were completely open with each other, all the time, about everything. Love didn't have secrets. OK, maybe they had never actually discussed the subject, but it had never seemed to be necessary. She had always been open with Titus and she took it for granted that he had been the same with her. When Titus came home he strode into the house, grabbed her, and hugged her fiercely, telling her how much he loved and had missed her.

Immediately disarmed, Alys forgot to be angry and said coquettishly, 'How much did you miss me?'

Titus grinned, 'Enough to carry you up to bed and make love to you right now.'

She pouted, her hands going to his belt. 'You can't have missed me enough, then, if you can wait that long.'

His eyes glinting, Titus said, 'Now that, you wanton hussy, is a definite challenge.' And he went to grab her.

Alys gave a shriek of excited fear and turned to run but he caught her and began to pull off her clothes as she tried to struggle up the stairs. They got as far as the half-landing before she lay naked below him, trapped by his arm as he tore off the last of his own clothes. For a moment he grinned down at her, both of them enjoying to the full this moment of pre-sexual anticipation, their bodies hot with desire. Letting his hand wander caressingly over her breast, Titus said thickly, 'If you throw out a challenge you must be ready to take the consequences.'

Alys smiled, and let her own hand do some exploring. 'I *am* ready. And—oh! I think you are, too.'

It was over quickly, too quickly; they had both been too excited and eager for any finesse. Titus gave a great sigh of contentment as he rolled off her, then laughed as he saw where they were. 'I think this is a first.'

'Mmm.' Alys sat up, only now aware of the hardness of the floor. 'How did we finish up here?'

Looking up at her dishevelled mane of golden hair, its length reaching to curl almost caressingly on the whiteness of her firm, rose-tipped breasts, Titus said, his voice again thickening, 'Who said anything about finishing?'

'What?' Turning to run widening eyes over him, Alys said, 'Oh, wow! You'll have to go away *again*.'

They made it as far as the bed this time, a king-sized bed that almost filled the room. And afterwards, when they lay languorously in each other's arms, their energy spent, Alys's anger was completely forgotten.

Her head on his shoulder, his still unsteady heartbeat under her cheek, she played with the hairs on his chest, curling them around her fingers, as she said, 'Why did you go away?'

Under her hand she felt him stiffen and it was a few moments before Titus said, 'I didn't want to go. It was an old college friend who was in a spot of bother, and needed some help to sort it out.'

'And did you?'

'Yes, hopefully everything's fine again now.'

'Which friend was it?'

'No one you know; somebody I hadn't seen for years and had almost forgotten about.'

'Why come to you for help, then?'

He hesitated, as if choosing his words. 'Possibly because I could deal with the trouble best—and because I owed a favour.'

'What kind of trouble was it?'

Turning towards her, Titus tapped her on the nose. 'You are a very nosy woman, do you know that? Aren't I allowed any secrets?'

'No!'

'I bet you have secrets from me.'

'Of course I don't.'

'No? What about that new coat you sneaked into the house and think I don't know about? You deserve to be punished for that.' And he began to tickle her, knowing that she couldn't stand it for long.

Alys shrieked and ran away from him, locking herself in the bathroom, only letting him in to shower when he promised to stop. And it wasn't until a long time later, when it seemed completely irrelevant, that she remembered he hadn't told her what his friend's 'spot of bother' had been.

Soon Alys had forgotten the whole incident; she began to make more definite plans for the wedding in the spring of the following year, but first there was the long vacation to look forward to when they were going to Egypt again. And this time Alys was to go in an official capacity as Titus's assistant and secretary, her Egyptian studies having qualified her for the post. 'And keeping me happy in bed is a very big part of the job,' Titus warned her teasingly.

'I shall be a kept woman,' Alys remarked. 'Paid for my services.'

'You sound almost pleased.'

'Of course I am.'

'You'd be thrown out of the Feminine Liberation Party if the members heard you say that.'

Coming to sit on his lap, Alys put her arms round his neck. 'No woman would want to be a member if she had you to go to bed with.'

He raised a pleased eyebrow. 'Keep you happy, do I?'

'And some. I think you must be the best lover in the world.'

Titus pretended to frown and look menacing. 'Have you been shopping around?'

'I don't have to. There couldn't be anyone more wonderful than you; I just *know* it.'

Lifting a hand, he stroked her hair, his eyes tender as he looked at her. 'Sometimes I forget just how young and innocent you are.'

'I'm not innocent,' Alys protested, thinking herself very sophisticated.

'Yes, you are—innocent of the world and trouble. You're one of the fortunate few who've led a cotton-wool life. The only child of adoring parents, and now protected by me. Everything has always gone right for you. A dream world. Do you realise just how lucky you are? Sometimes I think I ought to push you out and make you find out what the real world is like.'

'I wouldn't go. You're my world. Always and forever. I don't want anything to change—except for us to get married and have children. And then we will be complete and we'll live happily forever and ever.'

Strangely his eyes shadowed for a moment and he frowned.

Putting her hand on his cheek, Alys looked into his face. 'Titus? What is it?'

He hesitated, as if about to say something, but then turned his head to kiss the palm of her hand. 'Nothing. Nothing to bother your beautiful head about.' He changed the subject then, and Alys forgot about it, except to feel mixed emotions at being fobbed off with such a chauvinistic remark.

They continued with their rather insular lives, working hard, being sociable, but eager always to be together. But then, almost two months after he had gone away to help his friend, there was a phone call late one evening. The phone was out in the hall and Titus answered it. Usually he left the door to the sitting-room open, but tonight, after he'd exchanged a few words, he pulled it shut.

'What was that about?' she asked, when he came back.

'Oh, just some of the usual college politics.'

He sat down at his desk and went on with the work he'd been reading, but when Alys glanced at him ten minutes or so later Titus was gazing into space, a grim look on his face and his hand gripping the pen he was holding so tightly that the knuckles showed white.

Alys's biggest fault was that she often spoke and acted impulsively; now she opened her mouth to ask him what was the matter, but for once she held back. There had been rumours flying round the university about cut-backs for some time, and only a couple of days ago she had heard that some of the lecturers might have to go. Perhaps that was what the phone call was about. Although she couldn't see Titus ever being made redundant, because he was so good, his work giving him an almost international reputation now. But most of the other dons were his friends; he would be just as upset if he thought that any of them were to go. She would wait, Alys decided; Titus would tell her when he was ready, when he was sure.

To anyone else, Titus would have seemed perfectly happy and normal during the next few days, but Alys sensed the undercurrent of tension in him, especially when they were at home and the phone rang. She put out feelers to find out if there was any more definite information about the cut-backs, but if there was the teaching faculty were keeping it under wraps; none of her fellow students seemed to know any more than she did.

Then, late one afternoon, Alys came home and overheard him talking on the phone, his voice sharp, almost desperate. 'But what good would it do, Camilla? You know I'd come if it would help, but Harry doesn't like me being around and Tim just gets——' He stopped abruptly as he caught sight of Alys, covering the receiver with his hand for a moment, before turning his back on her to say, 'I'll call you back later. Yes. Yes, I promise. Goodbye.'

'Who was that?' Alys asked in astonishment.

'It was...' Titus lifted a hand to run it through his hair, a habit he had when he was worried. 'It was the old college friend I had to go and see before. Unfortunately the problem didn't get settled as I'd hoped. I might have to go down there again.'

'Just what is this problem?'

A grim, fed-up look came into Titus's eyes. He went to speak but then the doorbell rang. 'Damn! That will be Bill,' he exclaimed, naming a fellow lecturer. 'He's giving me a lift to the faculty meeting and there's dinner at high table afterwards. I only dropped by to change.' Crossing to her, he put his hands on her shoulders. 'Look, there's something I have to tell you. Something I maybe should have told you before. But there isn't time right now so I'll see you later. OK?'

'What is it?'

But the impatient sound of a car horn sounded outside and Titus shook his head, frowning. 'I have to go.' He gave her a swift peck on the cheek and strode away from her, but at the door suddenly turned and came back to take her tightly, almost roughly, in his arms and give her a fiercely passionate kiss on the mouth. Then he was gone, with Alys staring after him and wondering what on earth had got into him.

Perhaps he had got the push after all, she thought with trepidation. Perhaps it had been decided to drop the chair of Egyptian studies completely, and that was what he had to tell her. But he'd also spoken about his friend's problems recurring. Was that what he was going to tell her about? After a few minutes' thought, Alys decided that it couldn't possibly be; it must be something about his job.

She cooked herself a meal, eating it while going through the notes she'd taken that day. At seven the phone rang, but when she answered it and said the number the caller cut off. Half an hour later the same thing happened. Alys was beginning to think it was someone playing a joke, and was ready to give the caller a rocket if it happened again. But when the phone rang for the third time someone did speak, a woman, and she

asked for Titus. There was nothing unusual in that—
Titus often got calls from female colleagues, students,
friends. But there was something about this phone call,
something in the woman's voice, that immediately made
Alys's skin prickle.

'Did you ring before?' she asked.

'Just get Titus,' the woman said tersely, rudely.

'I'm sorry, he isn't here,' Alys replied. 'Can I take a
message?'

'When will he be back?' the caller asked shortly.

'I've no idea.'

'Is he at the college? I'll call him there.'

'No.' Alys spoke quickly, instinctively trying to guard
Titus. 'He's at a meeting somewhere. Who's calling?
What is it you want?'

'I *want* Titus,' the woman said vehemently. 'If he
comes in tell him to call me at once. It's Camilla.' Adding
shortly, 'Oh, never mind. I'll call again later.'

Alys slowly replaced the receiver, her eyes bewildered
as she wondered who the woman could have been. Titus
had no mother or sisters, no close female relations who
would have the right to ask for him in such brusque
tones. And any of his female colleagues from the college
or university would surely be with him at the faculty
meeting. She wouldn't even speak to him in such a demanding way herself, and no one had more rights over
Titus than her, his lover. Belatedly she remembered the
earlier phone conversation that he'd ended as soon as
he realised she was there. He'd said it was to do with
his old college friend; could this woman be the friend's
wife? Thinking back, Alys realised that the person he'd
been speaking to was a woman. Wasn't the name he had
used then Camilla? Yes, that was it. Other names had

been mentioned, male names, but she couldn't remember those.

Feeling strangely uneasy, Alys collected up her books and put them away, unable to concentrate on work. She decided to wash her hair and ran upstairs to the bathroom, standing under the shower because it was easier to shampoo it there. Beneath the sound of the water she was almost sure that she heard the phone ring again. She stood still for a moment, listening, but made no attempt to go and answer it. Wrapping a towel round her hair, she dried herself off and put on a robe, before going downstairs to listen to some music. But that, too, couldn't hold her attention. A thought was niggling at the back of her mind, something she was reluctant to bring out in the open and look at. Earlier she had been indignant that anyone should make such terse demands of Titus, that only she had the right to do so. Because she was as good as his wife. Well, OK, at the moment she was just his partner, but they did intend to get married. But that woman had sounded equally sure of her position, so maybe—just maybe she had once been Titus's mistress, too.

The thought brought Alys agitatedly to her feet. Pressing her fingertips to her temples, she tried to concentrate. Was this Camilla some old flame of Titus's he was trying to keep secret from her? But why should he bother? Alys knew that she wasn't the first woman in his life; he was far too experienced for that. He was over thirty, for God's sake, so it would have been very strange if there hadn't been other women in his past. But he had never talked about his past, not where women were concerned anyway, and Alys had never wanted to hear, never asked him. She knew, when she was being realistic, that it was silly, but she liked to believe that she was the first woman Titus had ever loved, physically as well as emotionally. He had told her so often, told her he had been waiting for her all his life, so that Alys had pushed all thoughts of other women he might have held in his arms right out of her mind. Their love was too passionate, too pure, for her to sully it with such sordid pictures.

And yet this woman must be out of his past. Alys tried to convince herself about that, to try to stay calm and reason that Titus would soon deal with it once he came home. In her eyes he was omnipotent, could handle anything that came along, and would probably laugh at her for being so silly, for letting her imagination run away with her. It was probably something very trivial, very unimportant. Nothing for her to bother about—to 'bother her beautiful head about'. Dimly she recalled Titus saying those very words after he'd gone away a couple of months ago. She had objected to the sexism in them, forgetting that he hadn't answered the question. Biting her lip, Alys turned off the music just as it reached a crescendo, unable to bear the noise, leaving the room suddenly empty and still.

Pushing her thoughts back to the first phone call that evening, the one she'd interrupted, she remembered Titus saying that somebody, a man, didn't want him around. Was Camilla married, then? Or living with a man who knew Titus and didn't like him? But the only reason any husband could have for not wanting Titus around was if—Alys's heart seemed to stop for a moment—was if Titus and this Camilla were having an affair *now*. Alys tried to look at this possibility calmly, but her heart, mind, all her senses screamed against it. It was impossible! No one who loved her as much—and as often— as Titus did could possible want or need to have an affair with someone else. And anyway her instincts told her that he wasn't the kind of man who would have an affair with another man's wife. He was too honest, too honourable for that. And they were too happy, too much in love for Titus even to look at another woman. Alys was completely sure about that, too.

But he'd said that he had something to tell her, something he ought to have told her before, and he had looked tense and strange, so unlike himself. Feeling suddenly very afraid, her confidence in Titus shaken for the first time since they'd met, Alys sat down in the chair to wait for him to come home.

But it was the phone that rang again first, its strident call shattering the silence of the room. Alys let it ring for a long time, but it went on and on. In the end she couldn't stand it any longer and grabbed up the receiver. 'Yes?'

It was the same woman, and she didn't bother to say her name. Her voice as curt as Alys's, she just said, 'Where is he? I have to speak to Titus urgently.'

'Why?' The word was a bold, insistent demand.

But the other woman said tersely, 'Never mind why. Just tell me where I can reach him.'

'No, not unless you tell me who you are and why you want him.'

Camilla laughed harshly. 'I suppose you're the student he's living with. Still keeping you in the dark about me, is he? Well, if you must know, he was my lover too, once. Look, I haven't got time for this. It's up to Titus to tell you, not me. Give me his number.'

'No, I damn well won't!' Alys retorted, too angry yet to be shaken by having her fears realised. 'Why don't you leave him alone? He isn't interested in you. Leave him alone.'

To her surprise Camilla laughed again. 'You silly little fool. I need him. And he'll always come when I need him. Because he owes me—and he'll go on owing me for the rest of his life!'

Stunned, her wits shattered, Alys muttered, 'But—but I don't understand——'

'Just find him,' Camilla cut in viciously. 'Tell him I want him and he's to come here at once. Do you understand that much?'

Alys put the receiver down without answering, too shocked to feel anything for a while, but then she looked down at her hands and saw they were shaking. Irrationally she blamed Titus; he should never have left her alone tonight, knowing that—that vixen of a woman was likely to phone. And how *dared* he let his dark past interfere with their bright present? She felt sullied by it, and suddenly the walls of the room seemed to close in on her, and she wanted out, out of the home she loved so much. And Titus was to blame for that, too; he shouldn't have given Camilla this number. And he should have protected her, Alys, from any nastiness. She didn't want to know. Just didn't want to know!

When Titus came home she was waiting in the sitting-room, pacing the floor in anger, and dressed in a bright red outfit that showed a great deal of leg, her hair newly washed and standing out from her head in a ragged halo of curls like a Millais painting.

'Hey!' Titus gave a whistle of admiration. 'I didn't know we were going out tonight.'

'*We're* not!' Alys snapped. 'Your ex-mistress rang. And please don't pretend that you don't know who I mean. She said it was urgent. She, Camilla——'

'Camilla?' Titus's face paled.

Alys stared at him, appalled at the effect the woman's name had had on him. But she gulped and went on angrily, 'Yes, she's been ringing all evening—a couple of times she even bothered to speak!'

'What did she say?' Titus's voice was unsteady, almost fearful, but Alys was too angry to notice or care. He ought to be thinking about the effect it had had on *her*, not about this other woman's troubles.

'That you were to call her at once. She didn't ask, she *ordered* you to. And she said that you owed her—and that you'd always owe her! So you'd better just jump to it and do as you've been instructed, hadn't you?' she added furiously.

She went to stride past him but Titus seemed to pull himself together and, reaching out, caught her wrist. 'Where are you going?'

'Out. And don't expect me to come back until you've sorted this out.'

'Look, I can explain. I intended to tell you tonight anyway; you already know that. You see, I——'

'No!' Alys interrupted fiercely. 'I don't want to know. That—that woman sounded evil. Just get rid of her, Titus.' Wrenching her wrist free, she made for the door.

Titus didn't come after her, but his face was white and drawn as he said, 'Don't be like this, Alys.'

'Why the hell shouldn't I?'

'Please stay and hear me out.'

Alys's chin came up, her eyes flashing fires of furious indignation. 'I've already told you no. Just settle this so we can be happy again.' And she marched out of the house, slamming the door behind her.

She met up with a group of friends, fellow students, who were also at a loose end, and they went to a disco. It was a place she wouldn't normally have gone to; Titus's taste in music was either for classical or jazz and she had largely come to share his enthusiasm, but tonight she wanted music so loud that it would blast her worries from her mind, flashing lights that killed the pictures in her imagination, and enough drink to speed up the whole process. They stayed at the disco until two in the morning when they were all pushed out on to the pavement, temporarily deafened by the silence after the noise.

'I don't want to go home yet,' Alys said definitely, but her voice slightly slurred.

'Let's go back to our place, then,' someone suggested, so they continued the party at a house rented by half a dozen students.

In university towns, whenever there was a party, however impromptu, somehow word would get around and before long more and more people would turn up, clutching bottles or beer cans. When the venue was absolutely full, they would spill out on to the pavement, then the neighbours either joined in or complained, depending on their mood. That night it was a good party; the police didn't arrive to break it up until almost dawn. Alys drank a lot of cheap plonk, danced with a great many young men who wanted to know if she'd parted from Titus for good and were very keen to take over, but ended up sharing a single bed with two other girls.

Around seven in the morning Titus arrived, went through the house turning over sprawling bodies, and, when he found her, slung Alys over his shoulder, took her out to the car and drove her home.

Alys didn't know much about it until he stood her in the shower, clothes and all, and turned on the cold water. She screamed, floundering about, not knowing where she was and trying to get out. But Titus held her in there until she was completely awake and shivering.

'Now dry yourself and put this on,' he ordered, pointing to a bathrobe. 'Then come downstairs.'

'Can't I go to bed?' Alys pleaded. 'I have a terrible headache.'

'Serve you damn well right. Come on, hurry up, get your wet clothes off.'

'You do it for me,' she said hopefully.

'If I get hold of you I'll give you the spanking you deserve.'

'Ooooh, kinky.' And she collapsed into giggles.

But Titus had lost his sense of humour and he shook her angrily, making her wet hair send arching sprays of droplets around the room. Her teeth were chattering from cold and his shaking her made her head ache even more, but it was the fury in his eyes that got through to her, driving some of the fumes from her dulled brain.

'All right,' she shouted at him. 'Leave me alone.'

'You'll get changed?'

'Yes. OK.' He glared at her and Alys was sure that he would have ripped her clothes off if she hadn't promised.

'Then hurry it up. I want to talk to you.'

He left her then and she peeled off her wet things but stood under the shower at full heat for a few minutes before drying herself off. She put on pyjamas and the robe, an old one of Titus's that enveloped her like a rug, then wrapped a towel round her damp hair and went downstairs.

'In here.'

He had lit the fire in the sitting-room, but the curtains were open, letting in the golden morning light. Alys blinked at it, completely disorientated timewise. She tried to remember what had happened last night but most of it was a merciful blank.

'Drink this.'

She sat in a chair by the fire and he handed her a mug of very strong, very black coffee.

'Can't I have some milk?'

'Shut up and drink it!'

She was silent, quelled by his anger.

'Did you have to go out and drink yourself silly?' Titus demanded after a few moments. 'Couldn't you think of an adult way of expressing your feelings?' She sipped the coffee, looking at him over the edge of the mug. 'Well, have you nothing to say?' Titus asked fiercely.

'You told me to shut up,' she pointed out, unable to keep a trace of smugness out of her voice, still more than a little tipsy.

'You little fool!' He took a menacing step towards her and for a heart-stopping moment she thought he was going to hit her, but then he clenched his fists. 'Did you have to go and get drunk last night of all nights?'

He sat down in the opposite chair and Alys stared at him, trying to gather her sozzled wits, trying to gauge his mood. He was angry, yes, but there seemed to be something more. Carefully, trying not to slur her words, she said, 'When that woman phoned tonight—last night, and—and started issuing orders...' She set down the mug and put a hand up to her aching head. 'I was so angry, so unhappy. I just had to get out, away from here. Surely you can understand that?'

He gave her an exasperated, incensed look. 'You could have stayed and listened to what I had to say, instead of acting like a schoolgirl who'd lost her first boyfriend.' He made an impatient gesture and ran his hand through his hair. 'I suppose I hoped for too much from you.'

'Yes, you darn well did,' Alys retorted, suddenly firing up. 'When that woman said that you would go on doing what she wanted for the rest of your life—then, yes, I had a right to go out and get sloshed.'

'She said that?' Titus gave a bitter sigh.

'Yes, she did.' Alys leaned forward, looking at him intently. 'Is it true?'

He didn't answer at once, clasping his hands together and bringing them up to cover his mouth as if trying to hold back words he didn't want to speak.

She was suddenly dreadfully afraid, suddenly very sober. 'Why last night of all nights, Titus?'

He got to his feet, paced the length of the little room, then turned again. He had always been too big for the house, but now he seemed like an animal in a cage, trapped and angry. Coming to a stop in front of her, Titus looked down, his face drawn. 'Something happened in the past, so long ago that I'd almost put it out of my mind. Perhaps deliberately; I don't know. But now I have to tell you about it.'

'Have to? Not want to?'

'No!' The negative was deeply emphatic. 'I hoped *never* to have to tell you, but now I have no choice.'

Reaching down, he took her hand. To give her strength or himself? Perhaps both. Alys gripped it very tightly as she got to her feet and faced him. Her hands trembled and she was dreading what he was going to say. He was so reluctant, his eyes so bleak. If it was something really terrible, then how was she going to bear it? Quickly she put her free hand over his lips. 'No, don't. I don't want to know.'

But Titus shook his head. 'You have to. There isn't any choice. Not now.' He squared his jaw. 'I'm sorry, I would have given anything not to hurt you like this,' he burst out. 'I know that it will upset you and spoil things for a while, but believe me, my darling, I've tried to protect you from it, but it was no use.' He held her hand in both his. 'I can only ask you to listen and then together we'll work it out. If you love me enough——'

'It can be worked out?' she interrupted, and suddenly gave him a wonderful smile. 'Then it can't be that bad, after all. OK, I'll listen.' And she took the towel from her head and tossed it aside, letting her hair fall in a tangled mass of curls to her shoulders.

The look of love he gave her then was overwhelming, but Titus said ruefully, 'You'd better hear first.' Putting his hands on her arms, he said, 'Alys, I have a son.'

He felt her go rigid, saw her face become desolate for a moment, then mask-like as she struggled to contain the shock. It was a major inner battle, but somehow she managed to say, 'Well, that's no disgrace nowadays. I take it Camilla is his mother?'

'Yes. It happened when we were students together. There was a party—much like the one you went to last night, I imagine. We were celebrating the end of our first year. We had too much to drink and, well—you can guess what happened. I went away to Egypt for the long vac. and when I got back I found Camilla—four months pregnant.'

'Did she want you to marry her?' Alys asked tightly.

'Yes, but I refused,' he said bluntly. 'I had enough sense to realise that a drunken half-hour wasn't a good basis for a lifetime partnership. We hardly knew each other and we were both only twenty. Neither of us had any money. She insisted on having the child, and I went along with that; I don't believe in abortion. I got a job as a barman at nights and her parents helped so that she could take her degree. Camilla said that she would have the child adopted but when he was born she wanted to keep him. Well, I agreed with that, too, but I'd got to know her well enough by then to know that there was no way I wanted to marry her. So her mother looked after Tim until Camilla took her final exams, then she went back to her home town.'

'It was over, then?' She gave him a puzzled look.

'Except for the maintenance I agreed to pay for eighteen years, yes. Or so I thought. I kept in touch with her, though—after all, Tim was my son. But a year or so later Camilla wrote and said that she'd met someone else and was living with him. They were going to bring the boy up together and she didn't want me to see him ever again. She said she wanted to start a new life, forget me and the past.'

'And you agreed?' Alys lifted a hand to his brooding face.

'I felt I had to. I felt I owed her that. But I made her promise to tell the boy about me when he was old enough.'

'And she said she would?'

'Oh, yes.' His lip curled for a moment. 'She still wanted me to pay for his upkeep, you see.'

'But without her husband knowing,' Alys guessed shrewdly.

'I've no idea, and it didn't matter. But she didn't marry the man; they just lived together.' He paused, and she almost felt him gather his courage for what came next. 'I haven't seen or heard from either of them for the last ten years. Until that time I had to go away; Camilla rang to say that she was having problems with Harry, her partner. She thought it would help if he legally adopted Tim, and she wanted my permission. She insisted that I go down and see her lawyer to sign the necessary papers.'

He stopped, unwilling to go on, so she prompted, 'But it didn't end there?'

'No. I thought it had, but it seemed that Camilla suspected Harry of having an affair and was afraid of losing him, so she'd just been using me in the hope of making him jealous. But it had the opposite effect; Harry didn't like me being around, and he especially didn't like Tim finding out who I was. I suppose he thought I was trying to muscle in on his position as Tim's father.'

'Did you see your son?' Alys asked, forcing her voice to remain steady.

A strange look of both pleasure and regret chased across Titus's features. 'Very briefly. He's grown into a fine boy.'

Alys let go of his hands, her face taut.

He hadn't noticed her withdrawal; there was something more he had to say. 'Things came to a head last night,' he said shortly. 'That's why Camilla kept phoning.' He paused, but Alys suddenly guessed what he was going to say.

'They broke up,' she said hollowly.

'Yes. I'm afraid so. Camilla said that the rows had got worse and that Harry had started taking it out on the boy, punishing him for the slightest thing, and even cuffing him a few times. I can't allow that, Alys.' His mouth thinned. 'Camilla's probably exaggerating, but I think there must be some truth behind it. Perhaps Harry did it deliberately so that she would leave. She'd phoned me before, but I tried to keep out of it, for Tim's sake— and for yours of course,' he added.

Oh, thanks, Alys thought sardonically. She'd been wondering where she came in all this. 'And now?'

'Yesterday he threw them out. It seems he wants to move his new girlfriend into the house. Camilla came home and found that he'd had the locks changed and her things packed and left out in the driveway. And he'd phoned Tim's school to tell them he wouldn't be paying the fees any more. So naturally she turned to me for help. You do see why, don't you?'

'Oh, yes, I see perfectly.' Alys was completely sober now; in fact her mind felt brilliantly clear. And she was far ahead of Titus in his story, could see in it far more than he had said, probably far more than he even knew was there.

'They were living in Harry's place, then?'

'Yes.'

'So now Camilla has gone back to her parents,' Alys said, hoping against hope.

'Her father is dead and her mother is working as a live-in housekeeper at a private house. They have nowhere to go.'

'But surely Camilla can get a job, find a room somewhere?'

Titus's voice grew sharp. 'Tim was ill a couple of years ago and needed to be nursed. Camilla had to give up the job she had to be with him.'

'The Social Services—a council house?' Alys said desperately, fighting for her future.

'I'm not going to allow my son to be brought up in a cheap bedsit, owing everything to charity,' Titus said on a positive note, a note that Alys knew there was no arguing against.

Her chin came up and her eyes looked steadily, clearly into his. 'And so?'

'And so I've told them to come here. It will give Camilla a chance to get over Harry. We can——'

'Here?' Alys's voice was high with tension. 'You mean to this town?'

His eyes met hers. 'No, I mean to this house, Alys. I offered to put them into a hotel for a week or so, but

Camilla said Tim was too upset to face that. She wants somewhere where he can be quiet, and——'

'You envisage this as a long-term arrangement, then?' Alys interrupted stiffly.

'No, just as long as it takes for Camilla to find somewhere else.'

'Is that what she told you?' Alys asked on a loud, jeering laugh. 'For God's sake, Titus, open your eyes! Can't you see what she's done? This is what Camilla has been aiming for ever since she saw you again. Maybe it was she who was getting fed up with Harry and wanted to move on. So she thought up a way of bringing you back on the scene—and liked what she saw: a college lecturer, successful, going places, still unmarried. And she realised she had the ideal weapon to get you back— your son!'

'That's ridiculous,' Titus said shortly. 'Look, there's more to——'

'No, it isn't damn well ridiculous,' Alys flared. 'She's on her way here, isn't she? To live with you. To share your house.'

'Our house,' Titus corrected. 'And you're wrong. I just want the boy to have——'

'Yes, your precious son. Her excuse for getting back into your life. Why didn't you tell me about him before?'

'It was in the past. I hadn't seen him for years and didn't expect to see him again. There seemed no point in telling you. I didn't want to upset you.'

'Well, you darn well have now!' Alys yelled forcefully. 'And if you think I'm going to share a house with your ex-mistress you're crazy. Find her somewhere else to live. Now, today!'

'It isn't that simple, Alys.' Titus caught her hand. 'I haven't finished telling you about Tim.'

'I don't want to hear!' Alys dragged her hand away, furiously angry now as she foresaw their lives being completely ruined. 'She's tricked you, can't you see that? If you let Camilla into this house you'll never get her out. She'll make life unbearable for me. She'll come between us just as she is now!'

'No, I won't let her do that. Never! But I have to let her come and stay here until I can find her a place I can afford.'

Alys stared at him, her chest heaving with anger, but struggling desperately to control it. 'All right. If that's how it's got to be. But just keep her away for the next week, then we'll be going to Egypt and she can have the house till we get back. That will give—Tim time to recover and they can——' She stopped, suddenly aware of the tension in Titus's face. 'What is it?' she asked with a great sense of foreboding.

His voice strained, Titus said, 'I'm sorry, Alys, the trip to Egypt will have to be delayed.'

Alys stared at him, appalled. 'Because of her, of Camilla?'

Titus gave a deep sigh, then said on a fierce note of bitter anger, 'Yes, damn it, it is. And there's nothing I can do about it, Alys, so please don't let's quarrel over this. I'm sorry. I know you were looking forward to Egypt—do you think I wasn't?'

Sick with disappointment, Alys said, 'How should I know? I'm not sure of anything about you any more. I thought you cared about me. I thought my happiness was important to you.'

'It *is*. You know it is.'

'Then *prove* it. Tell Camilla to go to hell and take me to Egypt as you promised,' she pleaded urgently. 'Say you will, Titus. Say you will.'

She tried to force him to say what she wanted by her own vehemence, by her own desperate need, but there was only a long, painful silence before Titus said heavily, 'Please, Alys, don't do this. I can't leave England right now. Perhaps in a few weeks...'

'Damn you, Titus. Camilla's wrong when she says that you owe her. You don't! It's up to her to sort out her own mess. Let the boy come here if you must, but not her. Not her!'

Titus reached to take her hands. 'It has to be both of them. You see, Tim hasn't——'

'No, I don't want to hear!' She wrenched her hands away, tears of mingled anger and disillusionment running down her cheeks. But it was for far more than the lost holiday that she wept.

He let her cry for a while, then Titus said bleakly, 'Sweetheart, maybe it would be better if you stayed with your parents for a few weeks. I'll sort something out and——'

'Maybe it would be better if I stayed with them for keeps,' Alys shot back. 'Maybe it would be better if I'd never damn well met you!'

His face hardened. 'If you'll just listen to me and let me explain. You see, Camilla——'

'Camilla! Camilla!' Alys shouted with fury. 'I'm tired of hearing about her. Can't you see that she's tricked you? I'm sure it wasn't just coincidence that she told you about Harry's mistreatment of your son just as we were going to go away together. Look at the facts, Titus. Think!'

He stared at her for a moment but then shook his head. 'It may look that way, but——'

'It is that way!' she yelled at him. 'Don't let her do it, Titus. Don't let her come here, come between us. *Please*!'

'It won't be like that.'

'Yes, it will. I know it will.' Alys put her hands on his chest, desperate to get through to him. 'I'm not going to let that happen, Titus. I'm not going to stay here and let her destroy us. You've got to choose. Her or me.'

'No, that's idiotic. If you'll just be patient for a few weeks until——'

Gritting her teeth, Alys got hold of him and shook him. Her eyes blazed into his, imploring but steadfast. 'Her or me, Titus.'

'It isn't a question of Camilla. I'm doing this for Tim.'

'He's part of her. You'll never separate them. You've got to choose. Put them out of your life again and come to me—and the children *I* can give you.'

A look of anguish came into his face and for a moment Titus closed his eyes tightly, his jaw thrust forward as if in pain. 'I have no choice, Alys. You see——'

But she'd stepped back from him, her face white. 'There's always a choice. But Camilla's blackmailed you into thinking there isn't. Well, it seems she's won. I'm not going to wait around until she destroys us.'

'Alys, I owe it to them to——'

'And what about me?' she cried out in torment. 'Don't you owe me anything?'

'Yes, of course, but——'

'But they come first. Then to hell with you!'

She went to swing away but Titus caught her arm. 'Alys, you're upset now and you have a right to be, but if you'll just give it time——'

'No! I won't spend an hour in this house with her.'

His face hardened. 'If you love me, Alys, you'll stay.'

'And if you love me you won't let her come here!' He was silent and she gave a bitter laugh. 'An impasse, isn't it? And we've both used emotional blackmail.' Suddenly she reached up and kissed him fiercely. 'I love you,' she said brokenly. 'I'll always love you.' Then she tore herself away and ran upstairs to dress and throw her things into a suitcase.

He came up behind her but she'd locked the door and wouldn't open it, even though he hammered on it in frustrated anger.

When she came out she was ready to go.

'Don't do this, Alys,' Titus said urgently. 'I need you. *Please* don't go.'

She had never seen him beg before, never seen such a look of entreaty in his eyes. For a moment her rage almost melted, but then she shook her head. 'No! I'm like you; I have no choice,' she answered shortly. And, taking the scarab ring from her finger, she pushed it into his hand.

As he looked down at it, something in Titus seemed to snap, and he snarled out on a rising surge of fury, 'Has it occurred to you that you're behaving like a spoilt brat who can't have everything its own way?'

Her face tightened and Alys fought back the tears that were all too ready to fall. 'Whatever you say.' She shook off his restraining hand and started down the stairs, lugging her case.

He didn't follow her, but shouted, 'Don't be a coward. Stay with me. See this through.'

The hall was tiny; Alys got the front door open and stood framed by the light as she looked up at him, her face already dark-eyed with sadness. Slowly she shook her head. 'No—I love you too much for that.'

Titus gazed down at her, his face white, and for a wonderful moment Alys thought that he was going to relent, but then he suddenly opened his clenched fist and threw the ring back at her. 'Go, then,' he yelled viciously. 'Get the hell out! Why the hell should I care when you won't even listen? I'll never forgive you for doing this to us!'

Alys stared at him, appalled by his violent outburst, then, infuriated beyond control in her turn, shouted, 'And I'll never forgive you for allowing your ex-mistress and your bastard son to ruin our lives!' And with a sob of rage she ran out of the house, out of his life.

CHAPTER FIVE

THERE was silence in the cabin when Alys finished speaking. She sighed, and gave an unsteady laugh. 'Not a very edifying story, is it?'

'Human relationships seldom are. But you were lucky to have found a man you loved so much,' Aunt Louise commented.

'Does that mean you disapprove of my leaving him?'

'I see little point in having an opinion on something that happened in the past. Did you talk about all this to Titus earlier tonight?'

'Not directly. There was no—warmth towards me. The opposite in fact. He called me a coward again. Do you think it was cowardly to leave him?'

Seeing that she wanted reassurance, Aunt Lou said, 'If you felt that you couldn't stay, then it was probably right to follow your instincts. Do you know what happened between him and Camilla?'

'No. When he didn't make any attempt to get in touch I tried to forget him. But I suppose I was hoping against hope that he would sort things out with her and come after me to take me back.' For a moment there was a tone of little-girl bewilderment and resentment in Alys's voice, then it hardened into bitterness. 'But he didn't, of course.'

'Maybe Titus was hoping against hope that you would relent and go back to him,' her aunt suggested.

Alys sighed. 'No, he knew I'd made up my mind.'

'Didn't he give you any hint about what happened after you left?'

'No, and I was afraid to ask. I did ask him how his son was, though, but he just said, "Well enough," in the kind of voice that shuts you out.'

'Is there anyone on the ship who might know, do you think?'

'I couldn't ask someone else,' Alys said in a shocked voice.

'No, but I could.'

Sitting up, Alys plumped up her pillows and leaned against them. She shook her head. 'I shouldn't think there's anyone.'

'Then we'll just have to find out from Titus, won't we?'

'You can't ask him, Aunt Lou. I won't let you.' Alys's voice sharpened.

'I wouldn't dream of asking him—but there are other ways.'

Alys was silent a moment then said, 'You're taking it for granted that I want to know.'

'Don't you?'

'I'm not sure. I mean—what's the point?'

'The point seems to me that you still haven't got over him,' her aunt answered roundly.

'Perhaps not. Perhaps I never will,' Alys replied, trying to keep her voice calm. 'But what difference does that make? We each feel that the other let us down so badly that we'll never trust each other again. I don't think that Titus even *likes* me any more. He—he gave me the impression that he despises me.'

'Love and hate are very close emotions, you know.'

'I thought I hated Titus at the time, but afterwards I realised it was just anger and—and humiliation that made me feel that way. I could never really hate him,' Alys said with certainty. 'I don't see how you can if you deeply love someone.'

'Perhaps not, especially with a love as all-consuming as yours. But sometimes love as intense as that can demand too much of a man and a woman. You wanted it all to be perfect, and I think Titus knew that and tried to keep it that way for you. That's why he didn't tell you about his son until he absolutely had to. And that's probably why you ran away—because you couldn't bear to have your dream shattered.'

'Maybe you're right. He said I was selfish.'

'More over-protected, I think. He should have told you from the beginning, given you time to face up to it all, helped you and reassured you, so that you knew you were together. Instead he poured it all out on your head at a time when you were feeling low and vulnerable, and expected you to accept it and be as strong as he was.'

'His fault, then?'

'No one's fault. Just bad timing.'

Alys laughed. 'You're a great comfort, Aunt Lou.' Her voice caught. 'You always were.'

'Well, that's very flattering, but if I'm going to continue to be a comfort, then I think I'd better get some sleep. Do you know it's almost three in the morning?'

'I'm sorry,' Alys said contritely. 'You need your sleep.'

'Not as much as I used to—but I do need *some*.' She settled in the bed. 'Goodnight, Alys. And try not to worry; these things have a habit of working out, I find.'

Not worry! Alys thought. As if she could think of anything else. She set her mind to working out what was best to do, and, against all expectations, fell instantly asleep.

The weather was even hotter the next morning. People appeared in sun-tops and shorts, exposing patches of white skin to the sun's rays. The pool was popular, the pool-side bar even more so. The passengers lay on loungers in the sun or the shade according to their inclination, but vacated them at nine and eleven for the two morning lectures on Knossos and the Minoans. Alys stuck close by Aunt Louise for these, but towards noon, as they were approaching Crete, Titus gave a deck talk on Heraklion, the port where they were to moor.

After lunch they all piled into coaches for the short drive to Knossos where they were met by local guides who took them round in groups. Alys was on the lookout for Titus and Gail, but saw neither of them. Jack Reed was on their coach, though, and would have merely nodded if Alys hadn't smiled and said good afternoon.

'Did you enjoy your hour alone in Hydra?' he asked her as they waited their turn at the gate.

'I didn't get the chance,' she answered lightly. 'Titus Irvine turned out to be a tutor at my old university. He remembered me and came to chat.'

'Oh, that's how it was.'

So evidently he had seen her walk back to the ship with Titus last night. Alys was glad she'd told him; she didn't like hurting people's feelings, even a casual acquaintance like Jack.

Knossos, the Palace of Minos, was a large and impressive site, with quite a large area that had been restored, so that you got a good impression of what it must have been like about two thousand BC. But for Alys there was no sense of peace and timelessness as there had been at Delphi, no magical sense of history. They were just very interesting ruins with red-painted pillars and some good wall-paintings. Maybe it was because they

had gone to Delphi early in the morning and had been
the first there; Knossos was full of groups trailing their
guides and trying to sort out their own languages from
those of other guides speaking at the tops of their voices
in German, French, Italian and Spanish as well as
English.

The sun reflecting off the white stone was intensely
hot and dazzled the eyes so much that it was impossible
to see without sunglasses. There were also a great many
steps and nowhere one could rest, so it was hardly surprising when there was a shout for Jack Reed, but it was
Titus and not one of the cruise directors who came hurrying towards them. 'An elderly lady has passed out,'
he told the doctor.

Jack turned to excuse himself but Aunt Louise stepped
forward and said, 'I'll come with you. She might be glad
of some female support.'

Titus hadn't noticed them until Aunt Lou spoke, but
he looked round, recognised her, and then his gaze swept
on to Alys. For a searing moment their eyes locked, but
then he turned away without speaking, putting his hand
under Aunt Lou's elbow as they hurried after the doctor.
Alys went to follow, but then stopped, deciding she
would only be in the way. She watched them walk away,
Titus in shorts and T-shirt, as tall and strong as a tree,
Aunt Lou in her cotton dress, straw hat and sensible
walking shoes, small and frail in comparison, but trotting
gamely along beside him.

It wasn't until they reached the museum in Heraklion
that Alys caught up with them again. But only Aunt
Lou and Titus were there, sitting outside at a table and
having a drink. They seemed to be chatting in a friendly
manner—far too friendly for Alys's liking. She gave them
an uneasy glance, wondering if her aunt had betrayed

her confidence, not on purpose, of course, but by art-
lessly saying too much. Titus could be very charming
when he wanted to be, and also very sneaky. Alys had
never been able to keep a secret from him; he had always
known and got it out of her. She strolled up to them.
'How's the poor patient?'

'Oh, hello, Alys. Jack Reed took her back to the ship
in a taxi. The heat was too much for her and she fainted.
And in a most inaccessible spot, too. They were going
to send for a stretcher to carry her to the gate, but she
was frightened that they'd drop her, which I thought
was quite justified when I saw how puny the two
stretcher-bearers were. She was rather a large lady, you
see.' She glanced at Titus and said admiringly, 'But Dr
Irvine just scooped her up and carried her out to the
taxi as easily as anything.'

Alys sat down with them and gave her aunt an old-
fashioned look. 'It's one of his party tricks,' she explained on a patient note. 'The caveman syndrome. He
wows them with it every time.'

'Well, it came in very useful today,' Aunt Louise said
firmly. 'I don't know what we would have done without
him.'

'Oh, well, if you're going to admire a man just because of his brute strength, then there's nothing more
to be said.'

Titus, a wry quirk to his mouth, said, 'Shall I go away
so that you can discuss me without embarrassment?'

'Who's embarrassed?' But Alys stood up. 'No, I'll go.
With any luck I should have lost the guide by now and
can go round the museum at my own pace. Will you
take the coach back to the ship, Aunt Lou, or would
you rather walk?'

'In this heat, I'll definitely take the coach. But you do as you wish, of course.'

Alys nodded at them both and went into the crowded coolness of the museum. The artefacts were beautiful, many of them frescoes taken from the Palace, but she couldn't help thinking how much better it would have been to have seen them *in situ*. It was a great condemnation of modern man that everything of value had to be taken away and locked up in glass cages. She was gazing up at a breathtakingly graceful fresco of figures leaping over a bull when Titus walked up to join her.

'The figures are of both men and girls,' he remarked.

'They let women take part?' she asked in surprise.

'Oh, yes, the ancients let the girls have their fun, too.'

'I wonder what it was like to live then?'

'Extremely uncomfortable, I should imagine.' He glanced at her. 'Looking for your ghosts again?'

'There aren't any here; not like Delphi.'

'I thought I was your ghost at Delphi.'

She turned to look at him fully. 'I think you'll be my ghost wherever I go,' she said shortly, almost curtly, then strode on to the next exhibit.

Titus stood still, watching her intently for a moment before he came after her, but by then Alys was already cursing herself for having given so much away. I'm indifferent, indifferent, she muttered in her mind, but it was hard, so terribly hard not to let her awareness of him show.

'Why will I always be your ghost, Alys?' he asked, his eyes on her averted face.

Trying to recover the slip, Alys laughed a little. 'Oh, please don't read into that something that isn't there. I merely meant that you—and everyone else—that I've known in the past, and have—moved on from, are ghosts that you carry around in your memory... Until you forget them completely, of course.'

'But you haven't forgotten me.'

It was a statement, not a question, and for a second Alys was tempted to deny it, but wisely said, 'That would be rather difficult, in the circumstances. You were part of my—growing-up process. I've put you down to experience.'

'And have moved on?'

She managed to turn and look at him, her eyes steady, even laughed lightly, although her hand gripped the side of the glass case they were standing by. 'Of course. I'm sorry if you think you ought to mean more, Titus, but I'm afraid you're definitely the past tense as far as I'm concerned. As *passé* as these relics,' she added flippantly.

It was meant to be rude, to put him off, and his lips thinned, but then Titus gave a rather crooked smile, and, lifting his hand, let it lie beside hers. 'Good, I'm glad to hear it.' Idly he let his finger stroke the length of her hand, slowly, delicately, but very deliberately. 'I should hate to think that what happened between us had embittered you in any way.'

Alys had forgotten what surging emotions could be awakened at just the touch of a fingertip. She felt like begging him not to touch her, wanted to snatch her hand away, but knew that was what he wanted her to do, to prove to them both that she was no more immune to him now than she had been before. But knowing it was some kind of test helped and she was able to reach across with her free hand, push his away, and meet his eyes as she said lightly, 'Sorry, I'm fussy about who touches me. Try Gail, why don't you?'

This time she walked on further, into the next gallery. Titus didn't follow her this time; perhaps he would have done but two other female passengers came up to him and asked him a question about an object in a nearby case. Alys looked back at the end of the room and saw him gesticulating towards the case as he talked to them. Feeling safer now, Alys grinned, wondering how much the two women knew, because Titus was no expert. He happened to look up at that moment and saw her. To her surprise he gave a rueful grin in return, as if he'd read her mind, before giving his attention to the two women again. That grin of shared understanding, as much as his deliberate attempt to awaken her awareness, left Alys feeling deeply disturbed, her thoughts bruised. She went on to the next room, but moving more quickly now, not wanting him to catch up with her again.

At the inevitable shop, Alys bought some postcards to send home, then came out to where the coaches were parked. Most of the passengers were boarding them, but Alys was used to far more exercise than she'd had in the last few days and she decided to walk, despite the heat. She set off but had only gone a few yards when she heard her name called. Turning quickly, Alys expected to see her aunt, but it was Gail who was waving to her.

'Are you going to walk back? You don't mind if I come with you, do you? Those coaches are so overpowering. I expect you find them the same.'

Alys didn't particularly, but didn't bother to say so. She had also wanted to be by herself, to try and sort out her thoughts and feelings, but it was evident that Gail was determined to talk to her, and it could only be about one thing.

'Let's go back through the town, shall we?' the other girl suggested. 'There might be some decent shops.' And she turned into a side-street.

Feeling that this conversation was inevitable, Alys didn't protest, but fell into step beside her. 'What do you want to buy?'

'Oh, anything interesting.'

'Presents?'

'Oh—yes, I suppose I could buy a couple of presents.'

But although she looked in several shop windows Gail couldn't see anything that she liked. 'That's the trouble with ports,' she grumbled. 'They're always full of tacky souvenir shops.'

The things in the windows had looked OK to Alys, but maybe Gail had different standards. She waited, not bothering to talk much, more interested in looking about her.

'It seems you're a dark horse,' Gail remarked eventually, in an accusing tone.

'Really? In what way?'

'You didn't tell me you knew Titus Irvine.'

'You didn't ask me.'

Gail gave her a baleful look. 'You know what I mean. I told you about him but you didn't say you knew him.'

'You said you'd seen a "divine man", I think you called him. You didn't say his name.'

'No. Well, possibly I didn't know it then,' Gail conceded. 'But why didn't you tell me you knew him at the welcome-aboard party? I saw you looking at him, and you must have recognised him. Anyone who'd met Titus before couldn't possibly forget him.'

And you've never said a truer word, Alys thought, suppressing a hysterical urge to laugh. But she said instead, 'There wasn't an opportunity. And, anyway, I wasn't sure if he—er—would know me.'

'Well, that figures,' Gail commented in supreme disregard for Alys's feelings. 'But he obviously did, because he joined you last night.'

'Yes.'

Irritated by her unhelpful tone, Gail said impatiently, 'Well? How do you know him?'

'He was a lecturer on Egyptology at the university I went to.'

'Oh, I *see*.' Gail sounded pleased. 'You only know him on a student-teacher relationship?'

'I suppose you could say that,' Alys agreed, remembering the long hours they had spent in bed together when Titus had taught her so many things in their wonderful world of sensual love.

'Is he married, do you know?'

'I have no idea,' Alys replied honestly.

'I shouldn't think so; all the other lecturers have their wives along to share the free holiday.'

'But he's much younger than the others,' Alys pointed out. 'Perhaps his wife is at home with—with his children.' She didn't know why she'd said it—to tease Gail, yes, but that was stupid when the idea hurt herself so much.

'Why, yes, it's possible. But surely you must have known whether he was married or not when you were at university?'

'I didn't hear that he had a wife.'

'How long ago was it since you left?'

'A couple of years.'

Gail gave her an assessing look. 'You don't look that young—and you certainly don't act it.'

'I'm twenty-five,' Alys supplied with a small smile. 'I had a year's sabbatical between school and university, and after I'd got my degree I stayed on to take a doctorate. But I—gave that up.'

'Good for you,' Gail surprised her by answering. 'Too much education seems to make girls very dull.'

'Titus is an academic,' Alys pointed out.

'I said *girls*. In men I suppose it's OK—if they look like Titus it is anyway.'

Alys laughed. 'Do you always go for looks?'

'Well, money comes in handy as well, of course. Still, if Titus is a college don I imagine he must be quite loaded.'

'He might have—commitments,' Alys pointed out.

She thought she had spoken quite casually but Gail immediately pounced. 'What commitments? What do you know about him?'

'Nothing; I told you.'

'Oh, yes, you do. Don't tell me our divine doctor has a past! How intriguing! Come on, Alys, tell.'

'No.' An idea occurred to her. 'Why don't you ask him if he's married?'

Gail gave her a thoughtful look. 'Maybe I will. Tell me; you're not interested in him yourself, are you?'

'Definitely not,' Alys replied, and gave Gail an innocent smile. 'I grew out of crushes on teachers years ago.'

They parted when they reached the ship, each going to her own cabin. Alys found Aunt Lou resting so went up on deck to read for an hour or so, finding herself a lounger between two that were already occupied so that she didn't have to worry about Titus or anyone else joining her. But in light of what had happened during the last couple of days it would have taken a really outstanding book to keep her attention. Soon she lay back and closed her eyes, going back over the day. She had been with Titus for only a short while, and yet the few words, the few glances she had exchanged with him seemed strangely significant.

He certainly wasn't ignoring her, which he could easily have done, but Alys wasn't sure if that was a good or bad thing. She had the feeling that between them things had to be all or nothing. From the moment she met him she had had it all; from the moment she left him there had been nothing. And now? Alys stirred, disturbed in her mind. Titus ought to hate her. Perhaps he did. But whatever feelings he had for her he wasn't able to control them enough to totally reject her, to make out that he didn't care. He had sought her out, not the other way round, and had soon made it clear that he hadn't forgotten, that his memories were still raw, in fact. But if he'd married Camilla after all, then surely he would have put her, Alys, firmly out of his mind.

As for herself, Alys was intensely curious to know what had happened to Camilla. Had Titus married or got rid of her? But what about his son? The boy had been Camilla's weapon, and Titus might easily have grown to love him while they shared the house, the house that had once been theirs. Alys wondered if it was partly jealousy of his concern for the boy that had made her leave him. She'd thought his love was all for her, pure and undivided. OK, she'd been ready enough to have children, but as an extension of their love for each other rather than for the children's own sake, a natural outcome of the emotions that had overwhelmed them from the very first moment they'd set eyes on each other. Last night she'd told Titus that she didn't regret that moment, and that had been true; she'd never regret it. But knowing Titus had put paid to her wanting another man since; anyone who had shown an interest had been compared to him and immediately become as nothing. So maybe

Titus had been right to say that she'd shut herself up in a kind of nunnery, away from men. She had known the best, and the memory of that would keep her warm through the long, empty years of her life.

After dinner that evening most of the passengers went ashore to explore the town of Heraklion, and, although Alys would have liked to go, instead she played bridge with her aunt and two other ladies until eleven when they went to bed. She hadn't seen Titus—or Gail, but the woman who had fainted, excited at being the centre of so much attention, came over to thank Aunt Lou and had been full of feminine flutter about, 'That nice Dr Irvine. So kind. So *strong*.'

While they were preparing for bed, Alys said casually, 'You and Titus seemed to be getting along well this afternoon.'

'Yes, he's a most interesting man.'

'You know what I mean, Aunt Lou.'

'Then why don't you say it? No, Alys, I did not let him know that you had taken me into your confidence, but I rather think you let him know that yourself.'

Alys frowned. 'I did? How?'

Louise hesitated, as if finding the right words. 'It was the way you spoke to him. You betrayed the fact that you'd known him really well. If you hadn't told me about him you would have been more circumspect, acted as if he were only an acquaintance.'

'Maybe you're right,' Alys admitted. 'It isn't easy to pretend.'

'So why do it?'

Alys turned to give her a surprised look. 'What do you mean?'

'Are you ashamed of your affair with Titus?'

'No, of course not, but——'

'So why make it a big secret, then?'

'I don't want everyone on the ship to know about it.' She held up her hand before her aunt could speak. 'You just don't talk about past affairs; it isn't done.'

Aunt Lou shook her head in disbelief. 'I just don't understand your generation, Alys. It seems to be all right to go and live quite openly with a man without being married, but once you break up it becomes a guarded secret, as if it was all very shameful in the first place.'

'It may seem like that,' Alys admitted. 'But there are rules. Suppose Titus fancied Gail, for instance; he wouldn't want me strolling up and greeting him like a past lover, now would he?'

'I think he'd prefer anyone to Gail,' her aunt said in such an ironical tone that Alys burst into laughter.

The next day was Sunday and Aunt Lou got up early to go to the service at seven. She wasn't a very regular churchgoer, but one of the lecturers also happened to be a bishop, and, as she said, it wasn't often you got a bishop thrown in with your holiday. Alys got up, too, but put on a tracksuit and went jogging round the deck for an hour. At first there was a mist over the sea, but this dissolved as the sun rose and she soon grew warm. Alys paused to take off her tracksuit-top and tie it round her waist, revealing the sports vest underneath. She ran on again, becoming surprised to see so many of the crew out and about on the deck so early. But maybe this was the time, before most of the passengers were around, when they swabbed the decks or whatever. Most of them gave her big grins as she passed and Alys smiled back, thinking how friendly the crew were.

After three-quarters of an hour, she stopped at an open area of deck and did her exercise routine, one that she'd worked out over the years to keep her in good physical shape, and which also worked off a hell of a lot of frustration. When she'd finished there was a ripple of applause and she looked up in surprise to see a whole line of crewmen watching her from the deck above. So *she* had been the attraction. Alys laughed, gave them a mock curtsy, and went down to the cabin to shower and change before breakfast.

Later that morning they anchored off the island of Santorini, disembarking in small boats that took them ashore to see the coastal town of Thera, set high on the cliffs. Aunt Lou, however, had been there before so she and Alys were taking an optional excursion further up the coast. Titus must have gone with the main crowd because they didn't see him until they were driven back to Thera to have a look round before returning to the ship. The little town was full of souvenir and tourist shops, especially jewellers, and it was through the window of one of these that Alys caught sight of Titus. He had his back to her and seemed to be examining some trays on the counter, but Alys couldn't see what they contained. But Titus was alone; Gail wasn't with him. So whom was he buying jewellery for? Alys wondered. Camilla?

It occurred to her that her whole life had been disrupted by someone she hadn't seen, had only spoken to twice on the phone. She had no idea what Camilla looked like, whether she was beautiful or ordinary, animated or quiet. Whether she had the power to win Titus back even though he'd once rejected her. But Alys had run away even before Camilla arrived at the house, hadn't even stayed to size up the opposition. And in so doing had left her rival a clear field, Alys thought ruefully. She sighed, suddenly wishing that she hadn't left quite so hastily.

Aunt Lou glanced at her and gestured to some tables with bright yellow cloths outside a café. 'This looks very attractive; let's have a drink.'

They sat down, some other passengers came along and asked to join them, and then Gail and her mother. Gail pulled a chair up close to Alys's, and, as soon as the older women were chatting happily, leaned close to say in her ear, 'Titus isn't married.'

Alys hesitated but couldn't resist. Putting her head next to Gail's, she whispered, 'How did you find out? You didn't come right out and *ask* him?'

'No, of course not.' Gail looked smug. 'I got my mother to ask the cruise director. And Titus is definitely single because the company offered to let him bring his wife and he said he wasn't married.'

'He could still be living with someone, though.'

'I thought of that and primed my mother first. It seems the company has no objection to a steady partner coming along so long as it's all very discreet—the couple don't flaunt it in the faces of the other passengers, kind of thing.' Gail gave a gleeful smile. 'So I shall look on Titus as a lawful target.'

'You would have anyway,' Alys guessed.

The other girl laughed. 'Oh, no—if he had been married I should have looked on him as an unlawful target! Which would have been even more fun.'

Alys shook her head at her and went to speak, but some sixth sense made her look up and she saw that Titus was walking slowly past and was watching them. Alys flushed, which made Gail look up, too, and give a small start, which completely gave away the fact that they'd been discussing him. Gail recovered first and flashed him a bright smile, but it was at Alys that Titus looked, his eyebrow raised sardonically before he walked on.

'Excuse me.' Gail got up to go after him. 'You'll be all right without me, won't you, Ma? See you back at the ship.'

Her mother could only watch her go and try to cover up her rudeness. 'So impetuous,' she murmured. 'So full of life.'

They all fell silent, watching Gail catch up with Titus and slip her arm through his. Alys expected him to cut the other girl down to size, angry at the fact that they'd been talking about him, but to her surprise Titus gave Gail one of his lazy grins and seemed pleased to see her. Looking down at her drink, Alys tried to quell the ache of jealousy in her heart; Titus wasn't hers any more, she had no right to feel this way. But heart and mind didn't always agree, and Alys's certainly didn't now. Was she going to be stuck on this boat watching Gail pursue Titus until he succumbed and they had an affair, for heaven's sake?

She set her empty glass down on the table and gave her aunt an intense look. Aunt Lou, immediately getting the message, looked at her watch and said, 'Is that the time? Oughtn't we to be making our way back to the ship?'

Titus gave a lecture that afternoon but Alys didn't go to it, instead sunbathing on the sundeck and swimming in the pool while she had it to herself. But when she came out Jack Reed was at the pool bar and offered her a drink. They chatted amicably together, Alys's hair drying into golden tendrils in the sun.

'Thought Gail would be out here,' Jack remarked. 'She doesn't usually go to the lectures. Who's giving it?'

'Don't you ever read the daily programme sheet?' Alys admonished. 'It's Titus Irvine.'

'That's why, then. She's got the hots for him.'

'And you, I think, have got the hots for Gail,' Alys responded, meeting him at his own level.

Jack grinned. 'I admit I have. Something cruel. That's why I keep drinking so much cold beer—trying to put out the fire.'

'Wouldn't you spend your time better by trying to get Gail interested?'

'She won't look at me while Titus is around. He's too damn good-looking and clever.'

'You think brains are an attraction?'

'No, but Gail does—probably because she hasn't got much in that line herself.'

Alys smiled. 'You sound disillusioned.'

'No, just realistic. But I go for the dark, exotic type.'

The complete opposite of himself, in fact, Alys thought, glancing at his very uninteresting clothes and his rather plain face. She gave him a contemplative look, was about to ask him something, but changed her mind.

Jack laughed. 'I can read you like a book; you're wondering if I'm married, or whether there have been many dark, exotic women in my life.'

'Oh, dear, was it that obvious?'

'You've got an honest face.'

'I'm afraid so,' Alys admitted, with such genuine regret that he gave a burst of laughter.

'The answer's no, and no. I'm not married and there haven't been many women—not that many, at least. I've always been too busy working.'

'GPs do always seem to be terribly busy,' Alys agreed.

Jack shot her a glance that was strangely amused. 'Yes, I suppose they are.'

'You're not in general practice?' Alys asked uncertainly.

But Jack turned to catch the barman's eye. 'Another round of drinks, please.'

'Hey, it's my turn,' Alys protested, and insisted on signing the bill.

When their little battle was over Jack immediately started to tell her about some fantastic cocktail recipe he'd made up, promising to get the barman to make one for her on their last night.

'Why the last night?'

'Because after a couple of those there's no way you'll want to go walking round ruins the next day. All you'll want is to be loaded on to a plane and taken home.'

'Sounds a killer. What's in it?'

'Don't ask.'

'Bad as that, huh?' Alys smiled at him and glanced round to see that the lecture was over and the passengers coming out on deck for their afternoon tea. 'Be seeing you,' she told Jack and went down to the cabin to change.

After dinner that evening there was a display of Greek dancing by two of the younger members of the crew, introduced as Ioannis and Adonis. The latter name made Alys smile, but as the men danced, their slim figures swaying and leaping to the traditional music, something of their inherent male arrogance came across and she could imagine men dancing like this back through the centuries. And their women looking on with as much admiration as she could see on a lot of the female faces tonight, Alys thought wryly. Her eyes wandered the room, looking for Titus, but she didn't see him until the display was over and she got up to move her chair so that Aunt Lou could get past. He was standing almost directly behind her, leaning against the wall, his hands stuck in his pockets, casually elegant in a lightweight suit.

Alys's heart did its usual jolt and she was sure that he'd noticed her, but Titus didn't even nod, just bent to speak to the group of people at the table near him, a group that included Gail of course, then went over to the bar to buy a round of drinks. Aunt Lou wanted to play bridge again and, although Alys didn't particularly feel like it, they had no one else to make up the four so she had no choice but to sit down and play for a couple of hours until the ladies said they were tired and the game broke up.

'Now where are we tomorrow?' Aunt Lou wondered to herself as they walked back towards their cabin. 'Oh, of course, Rhodes. Didn't you say you'd been there before?'

'Yes, on holiday with Mum and Dad. About seven years ago. You'll love it.'

They reached the cabin and Aunt Lou unlocked the door, but Alys hesitated.

'Would you mind if I went on deck for a while? I need to get some fresh air.'

'No, of course not, my dear. Here, don't forget to take the key with you.'

'Goodnight, then.' Alys kissed her aunt and ran up the nearby staircase on to the deck.

It was a beautiful night, the stars so bright that she felt she could reach out and touch them. A faint breeze lifted her hair but the air was still as warm as an English summer day. In the stern of the ship, near the pool area, coloured lights had been strung along the awning frame and the rigging, giving the ship a festive look—an old lady showing off her jewels. There were still several people sitting out there, having a last drink before the bar closed, but Alys sat on a lounger on the shadowed, empty side, wanting to be quiet and think.

Had Titus been buying a present for Gail in the jewellery shop back on Santorini? she wondered. Surely not. He had wanted to be rid of Gail—or had Alys just assumed that? But at least today she'd learnt that he hadn't married Camilla, which was a comforting thought. Not that it should be, of course, but somehow it definitely was. She felt that for the last two years she'd been living in a kind of limbo, at first always expecting Titus to come for her, or at least to write or phone. But when he hadn't got in touch she had tried to bury the hurt, tried not to think or feel. And to a large extent she had succeeded, living from day to day, always keeping terribly busy, until it had become a way of life: action always, feelings never. But meeting Titus again now had made her realise just how much she still cared about him, even though he had treated her so badly. And her body had certainly told her just how much she wanted him, too, when he had touched her, when she had looked at him.

So what am I going to do about it? she asked herself. Am I going to sit tamely by like some weak-spirited wimp—or am I going to forgive him and try and get him back? That was quite an enormous thought, one that had to be gone over very carefully. First: do I want him back? There's always the problem of his son, and Camilla, and—— *Of course I darn well want him back*! she realised fiercely. I was the most stupid, proud, egotistical fool alive to leave him in the first place. And I want him, want him, want him! She sat forward, her body tense and her hands clenched into determined fists. And I'm going to get him!

The violence of her feelings made Alys feel suddenly weak, and she sank back in the chair, laughing a little at her own vehemence. But the decision had been made and her resolve was strong. And oh, it was such a relief to have made it, to have acknowledged the feelings that had always been there, deep in her heart. She had behaved with angry impulsiveness when she left Titus, and should have gone back, or at least tried to see him again, as soon as her feelings had cooled down. But pride and a kind of hurt bewilderment had held her back, and then it had seemed too late. Maybe it really was too late now, but Alys made up her mind to try to regain the happiness she'd lost.

But how to go about it? She couldn't just go to his cabin, walk in, and say, 'I still love you. I want to come back to you.' But why not? Alys sat up again, her mind full of excitement. Wasn't the direct approach always the best? Besides, Titus might be too taken aback to say no. But she didn't have to be so direct; she could just say that she wanted to talk. Alys got to her feet, heart fluttering with nervous anticipation, then came back to earth with a thud as she realised that she didn't know Titus's cabin number. But then she remembered that when she'd gone to buy some stamps she'd seen a list outside the purser's office.

Her impulsive heart pushing her on, Alys hurried along the darkened deck towards the brightly lit stern and the stairs that led down to the deck below and the purser's office. The sound of music, turned very low, still came from the pool area but there was no sound of voices. Wondering if, by tomorrow morning or even within an hour, her whole life might have changed and she'd have found happiness again, Alys strode into the light—then stopped abruptly. All the passengers, except two, had gone. Titus and Gail were still there, and they were dancing in a small, cleared area. Gail had her arms up around his neck, but Titus seemed to be holding her loosely, almost casually, and they were talking. But he looked up as Alys appeared so suddenly, and their eyes met over Gail's head. Then he very deliberately lifted his hand to tilt Gail's chin—and kissed her deeply.

CHAPTER SIX

ALYS had never been kicked in the teeth before but now she knew exactly how it felt. She recoiled, every emotion appalled by what she saw. But then pride, and the feminine instinct to save face at all costs, came to her aid. Lifting her chin, Alys laughed, the sound lifting into the air and drifting away. She saw Gail start to turn her head, but Alys quickly stepped through the door leading into the upper lounge and ran through the silent ship to her own cabin as fast as she could.

When she got there she would have liked to bang around and throw a few things to get her anger and feeling of humiliation out of her system, but Aunt Lou was fast asleep, so that she had to creep into the bathroom to undress and then grope her way across to her bed in the dark. Her surprise at seeing Titus and Gail alone together out there had been nothing to her horrified consternation when he had kissed the other girl. But now Alys realised that the kiss had been entirely for her own benefit, and Titus probably wouldn't have done it if she hadn't appeared out of the blue. But he had certainly taken advantage of the circumstances, she thought viciously. But to what end? That question made her try to think more clearly. Was it to prove to her that he didn't care about her any more, that he was quite willing to accept any woman who threw herself at his head? And she had just been on the point of going to his cabin and as good as offering herself to him!

My God, Alys thought in consternation, supposing I'd walked into his cabin and found him in bed with Gail! Her mind reeled at the enormity of the thought. What on earth would she have done? Turned and run, most probably. Perhaps even apologised first. For a while her spirits were really low, but then another reason for Titus's behaviour occurred to her: perhaps he had kissed Gail simply to make her jealous. That idea made her feel better—but not much. Why should he want to do that? For revenge, perhaps? That thought was unpleasant. It might mean that Titus had grown to hate her.

The uneasiness of her thoughts kept Alys awake most of the night, and she'd had only a few hours sleep when she was awoken by the sound of the ship berthing at Rhodes at six the next morning. There was no point trying to go to sleep again; Alys looked out of the window and saw the early morning sun shining on the ramparts of the ancient walls of the city of Rhodes. Quickly she dressed and went on deck to jog and do her exercises for the next hour. The crew were busy this morning and she didn't have such a large audience, but several passengers came out to look at the town before she went below, many of them greeting her as she ran past them.

It was difficult to ignore someone Titus's size, but Alys managed it that day, going off to do her own thing in Rhodes and managing to avoid him in the evening. Her thoughts and feelings were still hopelessly confused, and she had no wish to face Titus until she'd sorted them out.

That night the ship sailed towards Antalya in Turkey where it was due to arrive at about seven in the morning, but Alys was up before six to take her usual morning exercise. They were sailing towards the east and the re-

flection of the sun, low on the water, was so bright that
it dazzled her. She ran anti-clockwise round the ship as
she always did, going from brightness into shade, from
heat into coolness, not bothering to count the number
of laps but timing herself from her watch. The crew were
used to her now and she wasn't such an attraction, but
the ones who were around greeted her with smiles and
calls of, '*Kalimera, kyria.*'

Alys waved back but kept jogging, her fair hair tied
back in a pony-tail, a glistening film of perspiration on
her tanned skin. For the twentieth time she rounded the
stern and ran up towards the bow, into the sun. Now
she could see the coast of Turkey in the distance and
glanced towards it without breaking her stride. She
rounded the corner—and crashed head-on into a man
coming the other way!

'Ouch!' Alys put her hand up to her nose, which had
received such a sharp blow against the man's chin that
it made her eyes water. 'I'm sorry, I——' She managed
to get her eyes open and saw that it was Titus. 'You!'

He, of course, was perfectly all right. Dressed in
running gear like herself, he was just standing there with
his hands on his hips. But running into him had been
like running into a solid wall.

Remembering the last time she'd seen him, Alys took
refuge in attack and said angrily, 'Why don't you look
where you're going?'

'And you were, of course?' he answered sardonically.

'All running tracks are anti-clockwise,' Alys pointed
out acidly.

'Really? I could have sworn this was a ship, not a
sports stadium.'

She gave him a look of distaste. 'I think you've broken
my nose.'

'Well, that will give the doctor a genuine excuse to get close to you, won't it?'

Despite the sarcasm in his tone, that remark revived Alys's spirits considerably. 'Don't tell me you're jealous.'

'I'm not,' he responded at once, and perhaps a shade too quickly. Perhaps he realised it because Titus added, with emphasis, 'I have other things on my mind.'

'I suppose you mean Gail—and not just on your mind from what I saw the other night.'

'Now who sounds jealous?' Titus taunted.

Annoyed at giving away her feelings, Alys snapped back, 'Being jealous of you and other women is hardly a new sensation.'

Titus's face grew grim, his eyes cold. 'You had no reason to be jealous then.'

'Do I now?'

Immediately he looked amused and she knew she had walked into a trap. 'You might well have—but that would depend entirely on...' he paused deliberately '...your own feelings.'

An ambiguous answer that made Alys want to hit him, and also brought a touch of fear to her heart. But she managed to give him a falsely sweet smile, shrugged and said, 'I couldn't care less.'

'Why mention it, then?'

'Why mention Jack Reed?' Alys retorted.

'Well, of course if you like having him following you around like a dog...'

'He doesn't follow me around. As a matter of fact he——' Alys broke off, thinking it might be better for her own self-esteem if Titus didn't know that it was Gail whom Jack preferred. Switching to attack, she said quickly, 'And if it comes to being followed around, then what about Gail? I thought she wasn't your type.'

Titus shrugged. 'She improves when you get to know her.'

'Which you were doing the other night.'

'Something like that.'

'Well, of course, if you want to make a fool of yourself over her in front of everyone...'

'Then what the hell has it got to do with you?' Titus said shortly.

Alys's chin came up at that and she blinked rapidly. 'Nothing, of course.'

'No,' Titus agreed. 'Because you forfeited any rights you had the minute you walked out on me—when you ran away from something you didn't know how to handle, instead of finding the courage to face it.'

Not wanting to talk about the past, afraid of it, Alys said quickly, 'That works two ways, If I want a—a holiday fling, then what the hell has it got to do with you?'

'Again, nothing—I just feel sorry for Jack Reed, that's all.'

'And just what does that mean?' Alys demanded, bristling.

'Because he's too human ever to come up to your expectations of an ideal, dream world, with roses all the way. And if he comes to really care for you then the poor chap's going to get hurt when you kick him out of your life. Not that *you'll* be hurt, of course,' Titus added sardonically. 'You're far too egotistical to feel any real emotion—and you're certainly too damn selfish to care about anyone's feelings except your own!'

'And what about you?' Alys shot back. 'You proved that you didn't care about me when you——' She broke off abruptly, not wanting to get on to dangerous ground. 'Oh, what the hell does it matter now?'

'It seems to matter to you.'

Her chin came up and Alys gave a brittle laugh. 'I'll admit it did at first. I was stupid enough to miss you. But when you didn't even bother to come or even phone then I knew you were too darn busy with your ex-mistress to——'

Titus's jaw thrust forward. 'You didn't trust or believe in me at all, did you?' he bit out. 'You didn't think I could deal with the problem of Camilla and not let it come between us. You didn't even think my love for you was strong enough to withstand something like that!'

'Well, you certainly proved that it wasn't,' Alys retorted, hurt not only by that past, but by seeing him with Gail.

'I was taking care of my son,' Titus answered forcefully. 'Something you would have known about if you'd bothered to listen, if you hadn't been too engrossed in your own feelings of injustice to care about anything else. OK, you had a right to be angry, even to leave, but you were so busy being indignant and hurt that you didn't give *me* the right to explain!'

'You'd said all I needed to hear. You hurt me too much for me to stay. But if you'd really loved me you would have come after me.'

Titus gave a curt laugh. 'Which is exactly what I thought about you. I hoped you'd care enough to come back, but I suppose I should have known that was too much to hope for.'

'Why, you——' Pushed into fury by the unfairness of it all, Alys lifted her hand to slap him hard across the face, but Titus saw it coming a mile off and grabbed her wrist.

They glared at each other, standing close, angry hazel eyes blazing into equally angry grey ones. But almost instantly Alys was aware of his nearness, of the muskiness of sweat on his skin and the lingering aroma of aftershave, of the strength in the hand that held her captive. A great tremor ran through her and the anger left her face as her eyes darkened. Titus made a small, surprised sound in his throat, but then they both jumped out of their skins as the ship's hooter, close above their heads, burst into sound as the ship passed another leaving the nearby port.

Immediately Alys wrenched her hand away, said, 'Get out of my way, can't you?' and ran past him, on round the ship. But she abandoned the rest of her exercise session and took the nearest route down to the cabin.

She found her aunt already up and dressed. 'Shall I go ahead to breakfast or would you like me to wait for you?' Louise asked.

'Wait, please. I won't be long.'

Her aunt gave her a searching look. 'Are you all right, Alys? You look rather upset.'

'Do I?' Alys hesitated, then said unhappily, 'I ran into Titus on the promenade deck—literally.' She put up a hand to rub her nose. 'We—we had a row.'

'Well, that was to be expected,' Louise answered calmly. 'When two people with emotions as raw as yours and Titus's must meet, then they're bound to rub sparks off each other.'

'Do you think so?'

'I'm sure of it,' the older woman said firmly. 'It's just what I expected to happen.'

Remembering that her aunt had engineered all this, Alys couldn't help giving her an angry look. 'Well, it isn't pleasant. As a matter of fact it damn well hurts!'

'Good!'

'Good?' Alys stared at her disbelievingly.

'Yes, good. You're having to confront your own feelings about Titus instead of burying them away. And once you've faced those, then perhaps you'll be ready to start living again.'

'I have been living,' Alys said indignantly.

'No, you haven't, Alys. Your parents have been very worried about you; they feel that you've just buried yourself away because you're afraid of being hurt again. Well, I think it's time now for you to come out of your shell and face your problems.'

'And you thought this was the way to do it,' Alys said a little sourly.

'I think it's the only way. Until you get over Titus you'll never be able to find true happiness and contentment with someone else.'

Alys lifted a strained face to her aunt. 'I don't want anyone else.'

'Then you'd better try to get Titus back.'

'It isn't that simple. I don't *know* how he feels about me. I don't think he wants me back,' Alys said on a desperate note.

'Perhaps he may not. But I'm sure that during this trip you will find out—one way or the other.'

And that was what she was afraid of, Alys thought as she stood under the shower. For a moment she longed to be back at the school where she worked, safe among that body of women and girls, where all she had to worry about was picking the netball teams and marking exercise books. A sanctuary where she could lick her wounds—or, in Titus's eyes, a retreat into cowardice. Looking deeply inwards, Alys realised that both were right, and she saw, too, that if she wasn't very careful it could easily become a prison of her own making. Aunt Lou was right, too: she had to face up to things, not run and hide any more. But that was proving very difficult, and Alys wasn't at all sure that she could go on.

She hadn't attended the lecture on the excursion they were to take that morning so Alys didn't know what to expect and didn't much care; she was far too busy trying to make sure that they didn't get on the same coach as Titus. This was difficult to do unobtrusively, though, when she was also taking surreptitious glances all the time to see if Titus and Gail were together.

But she didn't notice either of them and concluded that they must already be on board one of the first buses in the waiting line. Their coach, the last in the convoy, was rickety and old. It rattled its way inland, leaving behind distant mountains and taking a long, straight and dusty road through fields where flocks of sheep and goats were tended by women in peasant dress. There were gypsies in tents made from plastic sheets, and concrete irrigation channels beside the road where cows came to drink. They had set out early, but already the day was hot and humid, the windows closed against the dust.

They came to their first stop, the ancient ruined town of Perge, pronounced 'per-gay', and followed the usual procedure of being met by local guides, one for each coach, who took them round. The whole town had been excavated to show a stadium, theatre, market-place, baths, fountains, and colonnaded streets that still had the original paving stones. It was impressive enough to make Alys forget about Titus for a while, but then her own group had to pass the one that Gail was in and the other girl came over.

Taking hold of Alys's arm, Gail pulled her to one side. 'I want to talk to you.'

'I must stay with my aunt,' Alys protested.

'This won't take a minute.' But Gail waited until both groups were out of earshot before she said, 'Was that you on the deck the other night?'

Taken aback by the blunt question, Alys flushed and said, 'Er—when do you mean?'

'It was you,' Gail said with certainty, looking at her face. 'I was sure I recognised your voice. Why did you laugh?'

Seeing that there was no point in prevaricating, Alys sighed and said, 'I often laugh when I'm embarrassed.'

'Embarrassed?' The idea seemed a novel one to Gail. 'It was such a coincidence,' she said on an excited note. 'That was the first time that Titus had kissed me.'

'The *first* time?' Alys asked hollowly.

Gail's lashes flickered for a moment, then she said, 'Well, of course. You don't think it ended there, do you? Not with a man like Titus. And boy is he *some* man.'

'You mean that—you and he . . .?'

'Of course,' Gail said on an impatient note. 'And let me tell you, Alys, that a shipboard romance is everything it's cracked up to be. Titus is a fantastic lover. It was out of this world! And he's very experienced. I don't know where he learned to please a woman like that, but he——' Gail broke off to give a surprised laugh. 'Why, Alys! You're blushing! I didn't think women did that any more.' She gave Alys a look of growing amazement. 'Good heavens! You're not still a virgin, are you?'

Angry at the other girl's question, Alys said shortly, 'Have you ever thought of minding your own business, Gail? And I really don't want to know about—about your cheap little affair!' And she quickly turned to hurry after her group, the colour soon leaving her cheeks as she became very pale.

She caught them up, gave Aunt Lou a painful travesty of a smile, and stood to listen to the guide. But it was impossible to concentrate now. The thought of Titus actually making love to Gail tore her apart inside, making her feel almost physically ill. The fear that Titus had found someone new since she'd left him had often crossed her mind, of course, but it was one of the things she had managed to bury away, something else she hadn't faced. Probably because it was too enormous an affront to her own memories, which were becoming ever more precious when they were all she had left. But now she had no choice but to face up to it, now that Gail had thrown the details of his infidelity in her face!

Infidelity? Alys took the word from her mind and looked at it. Was that really what she thought—that Titus had been unfaithful to her? In a way she supposed it was, because she had certainly felt fully committed to him, as committed as any marriage vows would have made her. But if she'd been married to him would she have walked out on Titus quite so readily? And would he have dared, then, to bring his ex-lover and her son to their home? The group moved on and Alys with them, but her thoughts were a couple of thousand years away from the others. She had wanted to be married to him, and would have been if Camilla hadn't come along. But would it really have made any difference? Wouldn't she have been just as angry, just as devastated? It crossed Alys's mind for the first time that her walking out on Titus could have been a sort of challenge, a cry for reassurance, saying, 'Come and get me, marry me, prove to me that you love me.'

And what had Titus's message been when he had made love to Gail? Because he must have known that Gail wasn't the type to keep something like that to herself, that she had chosen Alys as a confidante and would be sure to pass on the triumphant news that she had made yet another conquest. The thought of Titus being just another name to add to Gail's list made Alys cringe in a kind of shame. Perhaps that was what Titus intended; perhaps he had taken this way to show her just how little he cared about her now. Was he, then, going to flaunt Gail in front of her face to add to his revenge? In which case he would be using Gail for his own ends, which would hardly be fair. Although, remembering what a wonderful lover Titus had been, Alys strongly suspected that Gail wouldn't care even if she found out; in fact, if her confidences today had been anything to go by, Gail was loving every minute.

The group left the market-place and walked up a hill towards the stadium, the sun hotter now so that they moved more slowly. Alys tried to push the picture of Titus and Gail together out of her mind, but found that she couldn't. Even when she'd seen them kissing she hadn't really believed that it had been anything other than an attempt to make her jealous, had in fact been secretly pleased because she thought it meant that Titus still cared. Well, now she knew. All he'd wanted to do was hurt. Which must mean that he really hated her. Had leaving him in the circumstances, then, been such a terrible thing to do? she wondered miserably. He certainly seemed to think so, although she had been sure enough in her own mind that it was the only course open to her.

They walked round the stadium with the guide and started a further climb to the theatre but Alys was so rapt in her own thoughts that she didn't notice that Aunt Lou had stopped until she called after her. Turning, Alys

saw that her aunt was standing with two other elderly
ladies, the pair that they usually played bridge with.

'Alys, dear, we've decided to give the theatre a miss.
It's so very hot. We thought we'd go back to where the
coach is and get a drink. But you go on and we'll see
you back there.'

But Alys walked to join them. 'No, I'll come with
you; I'm beginning to think when you've seen one set
of ruins you've seen them all.'

That made the three women laugh, but they chided
her on her lack of enthusiasm. 'You wait till you see
Ephesus,' they told her.

They took their time walking back and arrived at the
coaches as the first groups were completing their tour.
'Look, there's some shade under this tree. Why don't
you sit here while I get the drinks?' Alys offered.

They accepted willingly enough and Alys went over
to a drink-seller's stall set under a big umbrella at the
far side of the car park. The man took four bottles from
what looked like a refrigerator on wheels and Alys held
them to her chest, cold against the heat of her body, as
she fished in her bag for the money to pay.

'Want some help?'

She turned her head, saw Titus, and dropped one of
the bottles. It hit a stone in the ground, smashed, and
sent a spray of glass and cold Coke over her legs.

'Oh!' Alys looked down helplessly, for once completely lost about what to do.

The stall-holder gave her a filthy look and came round
with a bucket to put the broken glass in. Titus took the
bottles from her and put them back on the stall, then
picked up the man's chair and told her to sit on it.

She tried to turn away. 'No, I must go——'

'Do as you're told,' he commanded. 'You might have cut your legs.' And he pushed her into the chair.

Taking out a handkerchief, he mopped up the liquid that was trailing down on to her feet, his touch gentle. 'You're in luck,' he said after a couple of minutes. 'Just one small scratch and that hasn't bled.'

Alys was silent, looking down at him intently, her heart pounding, still sick inside. When she didn't speak, Titus glanced up at her face, and became still.

'Are you all right, Alys?'

She gripped the edge of the chair, her face working as she tried desperately to control herself, but then burst out, 'Do you really hate me so much?'

His eyes narrowed. 'Hate you? What makes you say that?'

'Was leaving you such a terrible thing to do?' Her voice grew bitter. 'You were much older than me, Titus; you should have known how I would react, that I wouldn't know how to handle it. She should have—have dealt with it without involving me.'

He still had his hand on her ankle and it tightened as he said curtly, 'You would rather I had gone on keeping my son a secret from you for the rest of your life?'

'You'd managed pretty well up to then,' Alys shot back. But then she bit her lip and shook her head. 'No. You had to tell me. I know that. But do you have to be this—this cruel to me just because you didn't like the way I reacted?'

'What do you mean?'

'She told me, Titus. Gail told me!'

A wary look came into his face. 'What did Gail tell you?'

'That you were lovers, of course. That you went to bed together that night I—I saw you together.'

'She—had no right to tell you that,' Titus said slowly, watching her intently.

'Didn't she?' Alys said bitterly. 'Isn't that what you wanted?'

'Why should I want it?'

'To hurt me, of course. You knew she'd tell me, and you—you just wanted to turn the knife.'

'And does it hurt?'

'Yes, of course it damn well hurts!' Alys's voice shook. 'I didn't know you hated me so much. That you could be so cruel.'

'And wasn't what you did to me cruel?' Titus demanded, his voice suddenly harsh and strange.

'How could it possibly be? You were the one who——' Alys suddenly broke off and got hurriedly to her feet as she saw the cruise director walking over to them.

'Everything all right?' he enquired.

'Thank you, yes. I stupidly dropped a bottle and Dr Irvine kindly lent his handkerchief to mop me up,' Alys said hastily. Somehow she managed to look at Titus and nod. 'Thank you for your help.'

She bought a replacement bottle while Titus gave the poor stall-holder his chair back, then headed quickly back to her aunt and the other ladies, gripping the bottles tightly, trying not to let the liquid spill because her hands were shaking so much.

'I'm afraid we'll have to drink out of the bottles,' she apologised. 'There weren't any cups or straws.'

'Well, I don't expect it will kill us,' one said tolerantly, but Aunt Lou handed round tissues and insisted that they wipe the neck of the bottles carefully before they drank from them.

Alys sat down beside them in the shade and watched as Titus carried half a dozen drinks over to some of his group, Gail stepping forward to greet him and putting a possessive arm through his as they stood together, a little apart from the others, their heads close. She couldn't have said more plainly, 'Look what I've landed,' if she'd stood in the middle of them all and shouted it out loud, Alys thought wretchedly. It must have been perfectly obvious to all the passengers that they were now lovers. As she watched, Titus turned to look in her direction and then Gail lifted her head and looked, too. Alys could only think that Titus must be telling Gail about her, about their affair, and Alys's humiliation was complete.

At last they were able to board the coaches and leave. Looking back at the ruins, Alys decided she never wanted to hear the name of Perge again, and was heartily glad to go. But the town had been only their first call and there was another place to visit before they could go back to the ship. It was only a few miles to their next stop at Aspendos, but the bus had no air-conditioning and many of the women were fanning themselves, so it was a relief when the coach stopped outside a building in the middle of nowhere, its front looking rather like an old, high warehouse.

As luck had it they were in the last coach that day, the one that Jack Reed, as the tour doctor, always travelled in. He helped Aunt Lou down the high step of the coach and smiled a little as he put out a hand for Alys but she jumped lightly down. They went through the entrance of the building, their eyes blinking in the shade, and then Alys realised that she'd been entirely wrong about one set of ruins being much like another as she stepped out into an almost perfect Roman theatre. The tiers of seats stretched high above them in a huge semi-circle, and above the seats there was a complete arched colonnade where the Roman traders had stood to sell their wares. Souvenirs and drinks, perhaps, just like any modern-day event. Alys turned to look at the stage behind her and caught her breath at the stone-columned walls with ornate doors and windows for the players to go in and out, at the niches for busts and statues. It was the most perfect ancient theatre she'd ever seen.

There were other people there today, too: ordinary tourists, and an orderly crowd of little Turkish school-girls in neat dark uniforms, their blouses and socks glowingly white, like soap-powder adverts. For a while all the passengers wandered around, exploring. Alys, wanting to be by herself, climbed to the top to look at the arched colonnade, but Aunt Lou didn't attempt it, so Alys sat right at the back, alone, when the passengers all gathered together again on the shady side of the theatre, sitting on the stone seats, waiting for a promised talk.

She hadn't realised that the speaker was to be Titus. He walked out into the sunlight to stand in front of them, in the exact centre of the orchestra, the circular area between the seats and the stage building, where players had first stood nearly two thousand years ago. A shaft of sunlight came through one of the windows, shining down on to the exact spot where he stood, bathing him in gold. Anyone else would have looked small and lonely standing there, but his tall figure and his presence filled the stage and brought everyone quickly to silence.

First Titus told them the history of the building, speaking almost normally, hardly having to raise his voice for them to hear because the acoustics were so perfect. He told the story well, holding his audience, and not only the passengers from the ship but other tourists who were sitting on the stepped seats to listen. And all the little schoolgirls, although they probably couldn't understand a word, had sat down on the other side of the theatre and were waiting politely for him to finish.

Titus came to the end of the talk and Alys expected him to walk away, but instead he gave them all a strange, almost ironical smile and said, 'Perhaps you would like to hear a piece of poetry, much as the Romans must have done—but this was written several hundred years later.' And he began, his voice vibrant, to quote:

'Let me not to the marriage of true minds
Admit impediments. Love is not love
Which alters when it alteration finds
Or bends with the remover to remove:
O, no! it is an ever-fixed mark,
That looks on tempests, and is never shaken;
It is the star to every wandering bark,
Whose worth's unknown, although his height be taken.
Love's not Time's fool, though rosy lips and cheeks
Within his bending sickle's compass come;
Love alters not with his brief hours and weeks,
But bears it out even to the edge of doom.
If this be error, and upon me prov'd,
I never writ, nor no man ever lov'd.'

Titus's voice lifted to the heights of the theatre and died away. For a moment there was silence as each person took the words into himself, then a spontaneous burst of very genuine applause filled the theatre. The children, seeing that he was at an end, clapped too, and everyone laughed to lighten the atmosphere and remarked on how well behaved they'd been. People got to their feet and

walked down the rows of steps. A few stood in the centre
and did their own recitations, but stopped after a few
lines, feeling self-conscious and inadequate after Titus.
After giving a brief bow, he had walked away while the
applause was still going on, not once looking up towards
where Alys sat.

Around her people descended but Alys sat on. She
was staring at the spot where Titus had stood, her ears
still full of his words. He hadn't looked at her while he'd
been speaking, had kept his eyes on the lower tiers of
his audience, but the sonnet that had once been
Shakespeare's had been meant only for her; Alys knew
that with absolute certainty. And each word, each sen-
tence of condemnation, had pierced her heart. She sat
very still, as set and cold as the stone of the theatre, her
hands gripping the edge of the seat as if to let go would
be to die. So that was what he had expected of her—a
love that would never bend or waver, a love that would
last to eternity. And she had failed him at the first ob-
stacle to be thrown in their path. Titus had had a dream,
too, and she had killed it for him. Today he had told
her so, let her see how it had hurt, how her leaving him
had left him disillusioned and bitter. For there had been
bitterness in his voice, not obvious perhaps to others,
but quite clear to Alys's ears.

And her heart, too, was full of bitterness—at her own
stupidity, at the anger and folly of youth, which had
made her leave him but had confidently expected him
to do what she wanted and come after her—what *she*
had been too proud to do. She should have trusted him,
believed him, known that he was only doing what he
was honour bound to do to help his son.

A great anguish filled Alys's heart, lacerated it, a despair so deep that she was beyond tears. She had asked

Titus why he hated her so much and now he had told her. She had lost him, perhaps from the very moment that she had walked out. Now his love for her was as dead as the dust of this dry country, buried too deep for him to do anything but despise her.

So it was over—for Titus. But Alys knew now that for her the real hurting had only just begun.

CHAPTER SEVEN

'ALYS? Alys, your aunt is worried about you. Are you feeling unwell?'

It wasn't until Jack Reed put his hand on her shoulder and gave her a gentle shake that Alys became aware of him standing over her, his face concerned.

'What?' She frowned and shook her head dazedly, like someone coming round from a faint. 'No. No, I'm all right.'

'You're in the sun here, Alys; let's move down into the shade.'

She got to her feet obediently, but suddenly everything swayed around her and she had to grab Jack's arm. Immediately he put it round her, steadying her against him. They stood still for a minute while Alys took several deep breaths, trying to control her senses.

'OK now?' She nodded. 'Good, then we'll go down the steps nice and easy, one at a time.'

She had been up very high and it was an awfully long way down. Her legs seemed to have lost all their strength and poor Jack had to help her, much as she often helped Aunt Louise. When they got to the bottom she said, 'I'm terribly sorry. The—the heat must have got to me.'

He gave her a shrewd look. 'You look more as if you've had a nasty shock. But you really ought to wear a hat, you know.'

'I've got one; I must have left it on the coach. I'm fine now, really. Thank you for your help.' But she spoke stiltedly and her face was very pale.

The cruise director came back into the theatre. 'Oh, there you are! The coach is waiting.' He gave Alys a look which clearly said, Not you again! but had to ask politely, 'Aren't you feeling well, Miss—er——?'

'An attack of vertigo,' Jack put in smoothly. 'She had to wait to be rescued. But she's fine now, aren't you, Miss Curtis?' And he emphasised her surname to put the cruise director in his place.

Alys nodded and managed a smile. 'Yes, fine. Sorry to keep the coach waiting.'

They hurried outside and Alys repeated her apology to the waiting passengers before sitting down next to Louise. The older woman gave her a brief but searching look, then took her hand and held it comfortingly as the coach pulled away and headed back for the ship. Aunt Lou was tactfully silent, not having to ask Alys what was the matter because she had already guessed; apart from Alys, she was the only person who knew exactly why Titus had quoted that particular piece of poetry and for whom it was intended.

It was over an hour's drive back to the ship, enough time for Alys to recover a little and go to have lunch with her aunt at the taverna-style restaurant on the promenade deck. But Alys merely picked at the food on her plate, unable to eat, her mind too busy.

After lunch, Louise got to her feet and said briskly, 'We must go and get our things together for our visit to the museum this afternoon.'

'I think I'll stay here, if you don't mind.'

'I'm afraid I do mind. I'm not going to leave you here alone, Alys. You wanted to find out what Titus felt about you and now you do. So you must learn to live with it. After all, nothing has changed.'

They had been walking along the deck, but now Alys stopped and looked at her. 'One thing has changed.'

'What's that?'

'I've never really looked at what happened from Titus's point of view, only my own. When I left I was so hurt, so upset that I didn't stop to think. I just acted instinctively. And I expected Titus to put everything right and come after me, beg me to go back to him. I didn't realise how much I'd hurt him.'

'When people love each other as much as you two did, then any hurt, any form of—betrayal would be bound to cut very deep. Don't you think so?' Aunt Louise suggested gently.

Alys lifted a tired hand to push her hair back from her face. 'There's only one thing I know; I've lost Titus. He hates me for what I did, and nothing will change that.'

She walked on then, but her aunt stood staring after her for a moment before hurrying to catch up.

Alys duly went round the museum with her group, but afterwards they could choose whether to go straight back to the ship or spend the rest of the afternoon in the town of Antalya. Alys would have gone back to the ship but her aunt steered her towards the other coach that dropped them off in a square in the town, overlooking the sea. Jack Reed had also been on the coach; he came up to her aunt and said, 'Miss Norris, I wonder if you'd be kind enough to let me borrow Alys for a while? I have to buy presents for my nieces and have absolutely no idea what they would like. But I know that Alys works at a girls' school, so she must be an expert on teenagers.'

'Of course,' Aunt Louise answered, without even looking at her niece. 'Girls can be so difficult, can't they?' She looked at Alys at last, saw her making a pro-

testing face, but only said, 'Don't worry about me, dear;
I'll walk round for an hour with these other ladies and
see you back at the ship.'

She walked off and Alys turned to Jack. 'Whose idea
was that—yours or hers?'

Jack grinned, in no way put out. 'Let's go and have
a drink.' He put a hand on her arm and led her across
the busy main road and down a steep, cobbled lane that
led to the old port. Here they found an open-air café on
the quay with a pleasant breeze off the sea that lifted
the fringes of the gaily coloured umbrellas.

'We must have something Turkish,' Jack declared,
picking up the menu. 'What would you like?'

Alys settled for Turkish coffee and sat back while Jack
chatted about the museum. 'What did you think of the
statue of Hadrian, from Perge?'

'I don't think I saw it.'

'That's strange; I saw you gazing up at it for a good
five minutes.'

'Was I?' Thinking back, Alys couldn't remember very
much at all about the museum.

'Somehow I don't think your mind was on it.'

'No,' Alys admitted.

'Something happened to you in the theatre back in
Aspendos, didn't it?'

'I suppose you could say that.'

'Do you want to tell me about it?'

'Did Aunt Lou suggest I should?' Alys asked drily.

But he ducked that one. 'Sometimes it helps.'

'Not in this case.' She paused, then said shortly, 'If
you really want to know, I was—forced to accept the
fact that the man I love no longer loves me—that I'd
turned the love he had for me into hate.'

'But you say you still love him?'

'Did I?' She looked down at her cup. 'Yes, I do.' Her eyes darkened with sadness. 'So very much.'

'And I suppose this man is Titus Irvine?'

Alys hesitated, then nodded.

'That explains Shakespeare's sonnet, then. I wondered why he chose that particular piece.' He glanced at her, hesitated, then said, 'You must have known him quite well in the past?'

Alys nodded, and gave a little laugh. 'I suppose you could say that. Yes. We were—very close for quite some time.'

'But not recently?'

'No. I——' she summoned up the courage to say the words '—walked out on him a couple of years ago.'

'And I suppose seeing him again revived old memories—old passions? So hearing him recite that poem must have been pretty devastating.'

She looked away, towards the sea. 'Yes, it was.'

Jack studied her averted face for a minute then gave a rueful smile. 'I don't seem to be having much luck on this trip, do I? Both the women I admire seem to be in love with Titus.'

Frowning, Alys turned back to face him, making a supreme effort to think of his problems instead of her own. 'Do you just "admire" Gail, or is it more than that?'

'It would be a whole lot more, given half a chance,' Jack admitted candidly.

Feeling really sorry for him, Alys said painfully, 'I don't think you have even that much of a chance, from—from what I've heard.'

'I see.' Jack looked down at the table. 'What you've heard from Gail, I suppose?' Alys didn't answer, which was an answer in itself, and he shrugged. 'Oh, well, it was a nice dream while it lasted. Look, let's have something stronger, shall we? I've an idea we need to drown our sorrows.'

They had a couple of drinks but neither of them was really in the mood, and after an hour or so they caught a coach back to the ship. That night Alys and her aunt made up the usual four for bridge but broke up to go to bed quite early. Aunt Louise tactfully didn't mention Titus when they were alone in the cabin, although Alys could think of nothing else as she lay awake long into the night.

Alys didn't bother to jog the next morning and didn't want to go on the excursion, but forced herself to do so and afterwards was quite glad she had because the scenery was beautiful along the coast road. She sat by the window today and gazed out at distant mountains, long stretches of white beach, and coastal parks, green with trees. She blinked as they went through tunnels cut into the rock, and put on her glasses to shelter them from the blaze of light as the sun coruscated off the gently lapping sea.

The site they visited that day was an ancient port, small but very beautifully situated on a small promontory of land. There were far more trees than on any other site they had visited, so that it was shady and there was the sound of birds as they walked the old paved streets to look at the aqueduct and the tiny little theatre. Because of the trees and the sound of the sea it was infinitely more peaceful here. Alys felt it and wrapped it round her heart. The daily programme sheet had said that there would be time for swimming, so she had put on a swimsuit under her dress. When they came to the water's edge, where shaped stones still formed a jetty, Alys simply kicked off her shoes, stepped out of her dress, and dived cleanly into the water.

She was a good, strong swimmer despite her air of fragility, and had soon swum quite a long way out. Pausing to tread water, Alys looked back at the shore. Several people were standing on the old jetty, watching her, Titus among them. He had lifted his hand to cover his eyes, the better to see. Does he think I'm going to drown myself or something? Alys thought bitterly. It was a thought that hadn't occurred to her before and she resolutely pushed it away now. With a show of bravado, she lifted her hand to wave, then, turning on to her back, she swam even further out, crying now, because this was the only place where she could be alone. But after a while, aware that time was passing, she turned and headed back to the beach in a fast crawl; she had already come to the attention of the cruise director twice; she didn't want him to have to strip off his trousers and come after her this time.

The thought of the rather pompous cruise director without his trousers suddenly made her giggle rather hysterically, and she was still smiling a little when she reached the beach and waded out of the water.

'Had a good swim?'

Titus's sardonic voice made her look up to see him standing next to Aunt Louise, who was clutching Alys's things. Giving him a brilliant smile, she said, 'Yes, thank you,' and went up to her aunt. 'The water was gorgeous,' she said, and touched Louise's hand reassuringly, taking away her worried frown. 'There's a towel and dry things in my bag; I'll just go behind one of these walls and change.'

She headed towards a broken archway with a mass of overgrown trees and bushes behind it, but turned in surprise when Titus said, 'I'll keep guard for you,' and followed her. But as soon as they were out of earshot his reason became obvious as he said harshly, 'Did you have to frighten the hell out of your aunt like that?'

'What do you mean?' Alys stopped and turned to look at him, lifting a hand to wipe drops of water from her lashes, drops that he mustn't know were tears.

'That crazy stunt you just pulled, swimming out so far that you made everyone worried. Just what were you trying to prove?'

'Nothing! I just wanted to——' She broke off.

But Titus wouldn't leave it alone. 'Just what?'

'It doesn't matter.'

She half turned to go on again, but he caught her arm. 'I suppose it was just an impulse; you felt like it, so you did it—without bothering to think about anyone else. Which is just about par for the course with you.'

Suddenly, gloriously, she was angry and indignant. 'Take your hand off me!' And she wrenched free of his hold. Putting her hands on her hips, Alys glared up at him. 'And just what right do you think you have to criticise what I do? You said I lost any rights over you when I walked out on you; well, the same went for you when you gave me no choice but to leave. So just go away and leave me alone, you—you big thug!'

She strode away from him, went through the arch and quickly dried herself and dressed. When she came out Titus was sitting on a low stone wall a few yards away, ostensibly making sure that no one intruded on her. Without giving him a glance, Alys walked back to join her group. 'What a long way out you swam,' one of the women remarked. 'You must be a good swimmer.'

'Yes, I teach swimming at a school, and I'm used to an Olympic-sized pool,' she explained, loud enough for several people to hear and pass it on.

They left shortly afterwards, and as they drove away from the site Alys looked back almost with regret; its peace had reached her and eased her heart a little. Even that short scene with Titus hadn't destroyed its peace, and she felt better able to face things now. 'Things' being Titus, of course. And Gail. Alys realised that Gail hadn't been much in evidence that morning. She said as much to her aunt.

'I have seen her, but she does seem a little subdued today.'

'Gail, subdued? She must be ill.' But there was no animosity in Alys's voice. She realised she rather liked Gail, who still had a touch of natural openness, despite her outward sophistication.

Glancing at Aunt Louise, Alys said, 'Were you really worried about me when I went swimming?'

'Who said I was?'

'Titus. He was angry about it.'

'Was he really? I wasn't aware of him watching me.'

'So you were worried?'

'A little, until you waved. I'm quite surprised that Titus should say I was worried, though; I'm sure I didn't show it. Perhaps he was just letting you know how he felt himself.'

'He knows I'm a good swimmer.'

'And he should also know how upset you must have been after hearing that sonnet yesterday.'

'He doesn't care,' Alys said dully.

'Is that what you think? I wonder why he bothered to recite it at all, then?'

But Alys knew; Titus had wanted her to understand just why he no longer loved her, despised her even. And perhaps he had wanted to hurt, to hit back for the hurt she had caused him. And today? Well, that had been simple enough, too. He was convinced that she hadn't changed, that her swimming out today had just been an impulsive way of trying to get her own back. And maybe he was right; Alys just wasn't sure of anything any more.

The ancient port was the only place they visited that day. The coaches went straight back to the ship and it set sail as soon as everyone was on board, spending the rest of the day at sea.

That night there was another gala dinner, the 'Thousand and One Nights', with an oriental menu and the waiters dressed in Arabic-style clothes this time. It was a long meal, six courses, with coffee up in the lounge to follow. The food was delicious, so her table companions enthused, but Alys didn't eat much and couldn't remember the taste of what she did try. The ship's band was playing in the lounge, as it did almost every night, although Alys and Louise didn't usually listen to it as the card-room was on the upper deck where it was quiet. That evening Alys expected to play bridge again but Aunt Lou said that she didn't feel like playing tonight, so the two other ladies went quickly off to try and find another pair.

'Are you tired?' Alys asked.

'Not really. I just thought I'd like a change. The band are quite good, aren't they?'

Alys agreed that they were and sat back in her armchair. She was glad not to be playing bridge and felt nervously tense rather than tired. She was young and fit enough to withstand the loss of a couple of nights' sleep, but the lack of it had made her face fine-drawn and there were dark smudges around her eyes. Gail came into the lounge with her mother, but they went to sit over the other side of the room. Other passengers finished dinner and drifted in, the free wine they'd drunk making them louder than usual, and they'd made friendships by now, so were more at ease with one another, laughing a lot. Then Titus came in with a couple of the lecturers and their wives, and—Alys was quite surprised to see—with Jack Reed.

'May we join you?'

Dragging her gaze from Titus's back, Alys automatically smiled up at the two women who were hovering over the empty seats at their table. Soon they were chatting amiably with Aunt Lou, although Alys only sat silently and listened. Why do women always seek out other women? she wondered. Why do they never go up to men who are sitting alone and plonk themselves down with them? Because they've been brain-washed to think it fast, she supposed. And perhaps they were afraid that the men might be married. There were certainly a lot more women than men on board, although there were a few men on their own. But they seemed to single each other out, too, so perhaps it worked both ways.

'Such a wonderful doctor.' The words, spoken by one of the women, caught Alys's attention. 'He was absolutely brilliant at treating my sister. Everyone else she saw just said it was her nerves until she saw Dr Reed and he made the correct diagnosis.'

'Has he a private clinic?' Aunt Lou asked.

'Yes, he has, but he takes National Health patients, too, of course. And spends just as much time with them as the private patients, I understand. And he works *terribly* hard, because he's such an expert in his field. That's why I was so pleased to see him here,' the woman en-

thused. 'If anyone needs a holiday it's Dr Reed—
although it should be Mr Reed as he's a consultant, of
course.'

'I should imagine he ought to be able to afford to pay
for a holiday, then,' Alys remarked, becoming interested.

'Well, of course he can. He's quite rich, you know.
His grandfather built up a very big business, and his
father was in merchant banking.' The woman leaned
forward and lowered her voice to speak confidentially.
'I understand they left him a fortune, a very large
fortune. My sister said that he endowed a wing of the
hospital where she was treated, and helps to keep it
running in these straitened times.'

Well, the dark horse! Alys thought in some
amusement. And here's me been feeling sorry for Jack
because I thought he was out of work.

The woman's voice broke off abruptly and Alys looked
up to see Jack himself walking over to them. He smiled
a lazy greeting and the woman, flustered, said, 'Oh, Mr
Reed, we were just talking about you—but you'd rather
that it was *Dr* Reed on this trip, wouldn't you?' And she
gave a girlish simper, as if she was sharing a secret with
him.

He didn't answer, just held out a hand to Alys and
said, 'No bridge tonight? Come and shuffle round the
floor with me, then, although I warn you I'm no good
at it.'

Actually he was quite good; he moved well with the
rhythm, although he didn't try any fancy stuff.

'What was that old busybody saying about me?' he
demanded crossly.

'The truth about your murky past. The words "brilliant" and "wonderful" came into it quite a lot. It seems

you cured her sister of something highly mysterious. You're her big hero.'

Jack grinned. 'Well, at least I've got one woman Titus hasn't!'

'Why didn't you tell me you were rich and famous?'

Throwing his head back like a tragedy actor, Jack said in affected tones, 'I wanted to be loved for what I am!' Then in his normal voice, 'Not that anyone ever does, of course.'

'Thought you said you were always too busy to find anyone.'

'True.'

His eyes swept over towards where Gail was sitting, and Alys, following his eyes, said, 'Gail isn't with Titus tonight.'

'No, I noticed that, too. Why do you think it is?'

'I've no idea.'

His voice hardening a little, Jack said, 'I shouldn't have thought he was the type to taste and toss aside.'

'He isn't.'

Something in Alys's voice made him look at her and say quickly, 'Sorry! How are *you* feeling today?'

'Oh, I'm fine.' But her voice was brittle.

'I hear you swam halfway back to Greece this morning.'

'Couldn't resist using up some energy.'

'Was that the only reason?'

'Is this a free consultation?'

'Is that your way of telling me I'm to mind my own business?' Jack asked mildly.

'Would it do any good?'

'Shouldn't think so. I'm incurably nosy. In the circumstances I should think it was the only place you could find where you would be certain of being alone so that you could have a damn good cry.'

Alys gave him an old-fashioned look. 'I don't like men who understand women that well.'

'Sorry.' The music ended and they came to a stop. 'Come and have a drink. It's all right; your aunt is having a comfortable chat with the old biddies.' Taking her arm, he led her over to the bar, but that was only a yard or so from where Titus was standing with his friends. 'What would you like?'

'Well, as you're so rich, I'll have something extremely exotic, please.'

'Brazen hussy. How about a Harvey Wallbanger?'

'Sounds good.'

She stood to one side, waiting while Jack ordered the drinks, her back turned as much as possible to Titus and his group, and pretending an absorbed interest in a picture on the wall. But she instinctively knew that he was aware of her presence and was watching her. It took a great deal of effort not to turn and meet his eyes, but somehow Alys managed it, although she greeted Jack with a relieved smile.

'Here, is that exotic enough for you? I told them to stick lots of fruit and one of those silly little paper parasols in it for you, as well as a swizzle-stick.'

Alys laughed. 'How vulgar! It's perfect. Thanks. Did it cost a great deal of money?'

'Definitely.'

'Good! Shall we go outside?' Alys suggested, wanting to be away from Titus's disturbing nearness.

They wandered out on to the deck and leaned against the rail, sipping their drinks. To their right they could see the lights on the Turkish coast as the ship sailed steadily on.

'Why are you annoyed with me for not telling you I'm a consultant?' Jack asked.

'I was sorry for you. I thought you were a poor, out-of-work doctor. You aroused my maternal instincts.'

'Good grief!' Jack exclaimed. 'No wonder I can't get a woman.'

Alys gave him an assessing look. 'Somehow I don't think that's true. Women are always falling in love with their doctors.'

'Ah, but do their doctors always fall in love with *them*?'

They were silent for a moment but it was obvious where their thoughts lay, and Alys said, 'Why don't you ask Gail to dance? Singling me out isn't going to help you.'

'Does it help you?'

Alys smiled a little. 'Yes, of course it does—but I'm a lost cause.'

'And you think I'm not?'

'Of course not!'

'You're a terrible liar, Alys. Tell you what; how about if we get married so that we can comfort each other in our old age?'

She gave a burst of laughter just as someone else walked up to them. Alys saw Jack stiffen and she turned, expecting to see Titus. But it was Gail, and she was alone.

'There you are, Alys,' she said airily. 'I've been looking all over the place for you.'

As everyone in the lounge must have seen them walk out on to the deck, this was a little hard to believe, but Alys knew a cue when she heard it and said, 'Hello, Gail. How can I help you?'

'I want to talk to you—alone.' And she gave Jack a compelling look.

'I have no secrets from Jack,' Alys said mildly.

'Really?' Gail looked both amazed and intrigued, giving them a speculative look. 'Well, I have—so if you wouldn't mind, Jack, dear...'

'Of course. Would you like a drink?'

'Yes, please.' She glanced at Alys's glass. 'What on earth is that?'

'A Harvey Wallbanger. Would you like one?'

Gail shuddered. 'No, thanks, I'll just have a G and T.'

When he'd gone, Gail said haughtily, 'If I'd known you were going to betray my confidence, Alys, I wouldn't have confided in you in the first place.'

'That sounds reasonable,' Alys replied.

'There's no need to be clever!' Gail snapped. 'You told Titus that I'd told you we were——' she hesitated '—that we were close.'

'You told me you were lovers,' Alys said bluntly. She gave Gail an assessing look. 'Was Titus angry with you for telling me? Have you had a row about it?'

'Certainly not!' Gail answered shortly.

'Why have the two of you kept apart today, then?'

'Simply because Titus wants to protect my reputation,' Gail said loftily. 'He's afraid that people will talk if we're together all the time.' Her voice sharpened. 'There's no need to look like that, Alys. It's perfectly true.'

'Well, as he works in a university I can understand that he might be worried about *his* reputation,' Alys conceded. 'But I really thought that you were an enlightened feminist, Gail, that you were above all this traditional, establishment way of thinking.'

Not knowing quite how to take this, and not wanting Alys to lower her estimation of her, Gail said, 'Well, I am, of course, but Titus has these old-fashioned ideas about women, and he's very protective.' Belatedly realising that she had been side-tracked, Gail went on in a sterner voice, 'You shouldn't have told him, Alys. Why did you?'

'I don't know, really. It just sort of—came up in the conversation.'

'I didn't know you knew him well enough to have that kind of a conversation!'

She was about to go on but Jack tentatively put his head out of the door. 'Would you like your drink now, Gail?'

She gave an impatient sigh, but waved him on, saying, 'Yes. Yes, all right. Thanks.' She took a drink, appeared to remember something, and said, 'Oh, by the way, Alys, my mother has decided that it will be too tiring for her to take the whole-day trip tomorrow, so she's just going to Ephesus in the afternoon. So I thought I'd keep you company tomorrow morning.'

Alys smiled inwardly at the way she'd put it, but said, 'That's kind of you, Gail, but my aunt is taking the whole trip, so I'll be with her.' An idea occurred to her and, without thinking, she said, 'Perhaps you could keep Jack company, though?' Then, realising that they might both resent her intrusion, added, to give Gail a get-out, 'That's if you don't mind sitting in the last coach of course; poor Jack always has to travel in it.'

There was a perceptible pause while Gail weighed up the advantages and disadvantages, but then she gave Jack a sweet smile, rather like bestowing a gift. 'Of course I'll keep Jack company. I wouldn't want to leave him on his own.'

Alys was relieved to see an amused twist to Jack's lips as he said humbly, 'Thank you so much, Gail.'

There was the sound of voices and quite a few people came out on deck while the band was taking a rest, Titus and his friends among them. Alys expected Gail to go and join them immediately and was surprised when instead the older girl stayed and chatted animatedly, albeit mostly with Jack, for quite some time before excusing herself. But before she went she gave Jack another smile and said, 'I'll be back shortly and then we can dance, Jack.'

They watched her go and Alys glanced at Jack, wondering what he was thinking.

'Do you think I'm going to be used to make Titus jealous?' he remarked.

Alys gave a relieved sigh, grateful that he'd realised. 'I think they had a row. Or, at least, Titus probably made a cutting remark and Gail got upset.'

'It must have been an *extremely* cutting remark, then,' Jack observed.

She gave him a curious look. 'You have absolutely no illusions about Gail, have you?'

'None,' he admitted frankly. 'But I still find her fascinating. She's so—feminine, so one hundred per cent female. Secrets, intrigues, pride, vanity, she's got the lot!'

'And you'd never be bored with her,' Alys guessed.

'Yes, you're right.' Jack turned to grin at her. 'How perceptive you are, Alys.'

But for once not perceptive enough to notice that Titus had come up to them. 'Would you care to dance, Alys?' She blinked, taken by surprise and not knowing how to answer, until Titus gave an impatient sound and took hold of her wrist. 'Excuse us, Jack.'

He led her on to the small dance-floor where the band were back and playing a slow number. He didn't mess around, taking her firmly into his arms and holding her closer than a chance acquaintance would. But then there were other couples dancing and there was little space, so maybe that was why.

'What were you being so perceptive about?' he demanded.

'What?' Alys tried to put out of her mind the thought that she hadn't been this close to him for a very long time and concentrate. 'Oh, you mean with Jack. We were—er—just talking generally.'

'Really?' He didn't sound as if he believed her. 'You didn't used to be very perceptive—quite the opposite, in fact.'

'Do we have to talk about the past all the time? Why have you asked me to dance?' she said quickly, not wanting him to pursue the subject.

'Does there have to be a reason?'

'Yes.'

Titus gave a short laugh. 'Maybe you are more perceptive, after all.'

'So why?'

'When you swam out yesterday, what was *your* reason?'

'To get some exercise, of course.'

'The real reason, Alys—and don't pretend there wasn't one.'

She looked up at him, trying not to remember how many times they had danced like this before, how often he had bent to kiss her neck, and the number of times that had led to their hurrying back to their little house to make love. But remembering hurt, and her voice was suddenly hard as she said, 'I wanted to be entirely alone for once.'

Titus looked down at her intently. 'So badly that you had to swim half a mile out to sea?'

'Yes!' She tried to think of an excuse and said unsteadily, 'Working as I do in such a closed community and among so many people, there are times when you have to get right away or you'd go mad. You have to be alone to—to recharge your batteries. And it's the same on this ship.' And when she'd finished Alys found it wasn't an excuse at all, but the truth.

'You didn't used to feel such an urge to go off and be alone.'

No, because I was at one with you, Alys thought. When I was with you I was complete and whole, and I needed nothing else. Her hand stirred in his, like a bird wanting to be free of a cage, and she lowered her head, afraid to meet his eyes.

'Did you?' Titus insisted.

She shook her head. 'No. But—things are different now.' They were silent for a while and Alys welcomed it; she didn't want to talk. If she closed her eyes she could almost imagine that they were still together, still in love. But sadness filled her when she thought that this would be the last time she was ever to be held in his arms, ever to be so close to him. A great wave of grief filled her heart for what they'd had and lost. Titus's fault? Hers? It no longer mattered. Tears pricked at her eyes but she blinked them back.

'Alys?' Titus had bent his head to try and see her face properly.

Dredging up what little pride she had left, Alys lifted her chin and said, 'Do you think you will go on seeing Gail after you get back to England?'

'Why do you want to know?'

She shrugged. 'Shipboard romances are notoriously fickle.'

He gave a mirthless laugh. 'From my experience so are the ones on land. As you should very well know,' he pointed out needlessly.

'You're talking about the past again,' Alys said shortly, adding, 'But then that's all we have, isn't it?'

'Is it?' he said on a meaningful note.

'Of—of course.' Alys was suddenly afraid to look at him, afraid to think.

'We have the present,' Titus said carefully, his eyes on her face.

She gave him a startled, half-fearful look, wondering what he was leading up to. 'Your present would appear to be with Gail. Perhaps even your future,' she said equally carefully.

'I don't think about the future,' Titus said with a shrug. 'And the present is big enough to hold more than Gail.'

'What—what do you mean?'

Titus drew her closer, his eyes glittering down at her, and she felt the familiar surge of longing, of aching frustration and desire—the need that only the other night had sent her running to him, only to find him with Gail. A need that had now to be conquered at all costs. But Titus, unbelievably, was saying, 'We were good together; I don't have to tell you that, do I?'

'N-no.' She stared up at him, her eyes widening.

He lowered his voice, bent to speak so that only she could hear. 'I have a large, comfortable cabin all to myself. Why don't we get together—for old times' sake? See if the magic still works?'

She gazed at him open-mouthed. 'The—the magic?'

'We used to strike sparks off each other.' Titus was watching her intently, waiting for her reaction.

Bright spots of colour came into Alys's cheeks. 'You're propositioning me!' she exclaimed in a stunned voice.

'Hardly! Not when we've known each other so well. It's not as if it was the first time. It would just be a—rather nice way of reliving an old memory,' Titus said with a shrug.

'Like playing an old record you'd forgotten you had?' Alys suggested, her voice dangerously brittle.

'Exactly! You've found the perfect simile.'

'Just to see if you still like the tune, if it still does anything for you?'

'Right!' He raised a suggestive eyebrow. 'Tonight? OK?'

After the love and sadness she'd been feeling just a few minutes ago, his open prurience made Alys feel suddenly defiled. 'If we weren't on this dance-floor,' she said fiercely, 'I would kick you where it hurts most! How *dare* you proposition me? I wouldn't go to bed with you, even if it wasn't the same bed you took Gail to.' She became aware that her voice was rising and lowered it to a forceful hiss. 'And for your information I don't keep old records that are no longer hits; I chuck them in the dustbin—which is where you belong!' And she pushed him away with a furious shove, abandoning him in the middle of the dance-floor as she strode back to her aunt.

CHAPTER EIGHT

THE cruise definitely wasn't for lie-abeds; by eight the next morning the passengers had eaten breakfast, listened to a lecture, and were making their way with local guides to visit the ancient castle at Bodrum, where the ship was docked. Then they boarded coaches again to travel to the next site.

Alys and Aunt Louise got on to the last bus, but deliberately sat some rows in front of Jack and Gail, because Alys didn't want to cramp Jack's style. And he seemed to be doing pretty well; although Gail had looked a little bored at first, Alys heard her laugh several times and guessed that Jack was doing his best to charm her. Alys wished him luck; he deserved to be happy. Her own emotions she determinedly buried, although she had spent another almost sleepless night, continually tormented by the thought that she could have been in Titus's arms. But not after the way he'd propositioned her, never like that!

They visited two more sights that morning, Titus giving a talk at the second, then drove to the shore of a large lake where they were to have a picnic lunch at a little café where tables were set out in the shade thrown by trees that whispered in the breeze. It was pleasant there, and after they'd eaten Alys sat back in her chair, eyes closed as she lifted her face to the sun. Then she felt the lightest touch on her shoulder and opened her eyes to see that a large, beautifully coloured butterfly had settled there. She watched, fascinated by its nearness, by its lack of fear, but then it rose a few inches in the air, to settle again on her lips.

By now several people had noticed and were watching, among them a botanist who was one of the lecturers. 'It's taking the salt from your mouth,' he told her.

Attracted by the small crowd gathering around her, Titus came over and watched as Aunt Louise took a photograph. 'One to show your grandchildren,' he remarked flippantly. At that Alys turned her head sharply to look at him, making the butterfly fly away. Wistfully she watched it go, brilliant against the clear blue of the sky, and when she looked towards Titus again he had walked away.

The lake was so beautiful that Alys was reluctant to leave it, but they had to board the buses again to visit Ephesus, the best preserved of all the ruined cities they had visited. Alys and Aunt Lou were duly impressed, but it had been a long day and they were glad to get on the coaches which were to take them back to the ship, which had travelled to another port to meet them.

They went early to bed that night and Alys was so exhausted that she slept deeply, waking only in time to catch the coach for the next day's excursion. Today there was a choice between a full or a half-day's trip, and Aunt Lou had chosen the half-day, admitting that two consecutive whole days in the heat were a little too much. But Titus, and of course Jack and Gail, had gone on the longer trip so Alys didn't see them until the evening.

She was up on the sundeck, reading, and catching the last of the sun when Gail came to look for her.

'You aunt told me you were up here.' She sat gracefully down on the lounger alongside Alys's.

'Had a good day?'

'Yes, I did actually.'

Alys gave her a surprised look. Knowing that Gail's mother had been on the half-day trip, she said, 'Who were you with?' quite expecting her to say Titus.

But Gail, looking a little sheepish, answered, 'Jack Reed, as a matter of fact,' adding rather defensively, 'He's quite fun.'

'Yes, I know.'

'And quite nice.'

'Very nice, I thought.'

'Well, yes. Nicer than I expected him to be at any rate,' Gail admitted.

'He has hidden depths, hidden talents,' Alys remarked, knowing that Gail would be interested in anything at all mysterious.

'What depths?'

'I expect you'll find out in time,' Alys evaded.

But Gail was becoming suspicious. 'Do you really know something about Jack or are you making it up?'

'I really know something,' Alys admitted.

'Well, why won't you tell me?' Gail asked.

'Because I'm sworn to secrecy.'

'Really? How intriguing.' Gail gave her a contemplative look, then sighed. 'I know your type; once you've sworn to keep a secret you'll never tell.' She shrugged. 'Look, you know we're not leaving this port until midnight? Well, I thought it would be a nice change if we had dinner in a restaurant in the town. I've already fixed it with your aunt; she says it's OK with her.'

'Gail!'

But the other girl had already stood up and was heading for the stairs. 'Meet you on the quay at seven.'

'Gail!' Alys shot to her feet and called after her as she ran down the stairs, 'Is it just the two of us?'

Pausing, Gail looked up at her. 'No, Jack's coming.' And she went on her way.

Inwardly fuming, Alys went straight to the cabin to apologise to her aunt, but Louise was quite content for her to go. 'It will do you good to have a change of company.'

So Alys dressed up a little in a white halter-necked dress that showed off her now deep tan and slim figure, and went carefully down the gangway in her high heels. Jack was already there, looking, for him, quite smart in a pale linen suit. He gave her a grin and a peck on the cheek.

'You look pleased with yourself,' she remarked, smiling back. 'How's it going?'

'Not bad. Not bad at all.' He looked up towards the gangway as Gail came down, dressed in glistening gold.

Alys looked too, and froze as she saw that Titus was helping her down. Swiftly she looked at Jack, but he didn't seem at all surprised. 'What's going on?' she demanded.

'Gail thought it would be more fun if we made up a four.'

'No!'

But Jack took her arm. 'Relax. Let's see what Gail's ploy is before you start panicking.'

'Maybe I don't want to be used as a pawn in Gail's games,' Alys said angrily, her voice lowered as the others came nearer. 'And I shouldn't have thought you would, either.'

But Jack only grinned and turned to greet them. Gail was buzzing and vivacious, full of excitement, but Titus read the annoyance in Alys's eyes and merely gave her a mocking smile.

'Let's go for a walk round the town before we eat, shall we?' Gail suggested. 'I'm told there are some super shops.'

They set off, Alys stepping in front to walk with Gail, the men behind them. 'Why didn't you tell me you'd asked Titus?' Alys demanded in a whisper.

Gail looked at her in surprise. 'He was the only spare man available. But you don't mind him, do you? I didn't think you knew him well enough to dislike him.'

Hoist with her own petard! Alys thought, realising how difficult it was to live such a deceitful life. 'I'd just have liked to know who was coming, that's all.' But Gail was already heading for the nearest shop.

The town was a fascinating mix of bazaars and modern shops. There were shoe-shiners with elaborate brass stands, each trying to outdo the others in ornamentation, sitting outside brightly lit jewellery shops. Boys carrying bathroom scales offered to weigh you for a few coins, while older, pencil-slim young men who were incredibly polite tried to engage you in conversation and lure you into the leather shops, full of the most beautiful coats and jackets. But above everything was the spicy scent of the land, which seemed to get muskier the further east they sailed. But it was never quite the same as the last place, and Alys thought that each piece of land must have its own particular scent.

'What are you thinking?' They had stopped so that Gail could look in a shop window and Jack had gone with her, leaving Alys and Titus momentarily alone.

Lifting her head to look at him, Alys said, 'You often used to ask me that. But then you really wanted to know.'

'Maybe I want to know now.'

She shook her head. 'I don't think so.'

'Tell me,' Titus said compellingly.

'All right.' Her chin came up challengingly. 'I was wondering what had happened to Camilla.'

Titus's eyebrows rose. 'You were thinking that? Here?'

'Yes,' Alys lied.

He didn't believe her, of course, but he amazed her by saying, 'I was wondering when you were going to get round to asking me that.'

Gail had been drawn into the shop to try on a coat, Jack following. Stiffly, Alys said, 'I'm not really interested, of course; it's just a—a loose end, that's all.'

'Of course,' Titus agreed smoothly. 'Camilla is married.' He paused deliberately and Alys had to use every ounce of self-control to keep her face passive as she waited for him to add, 'To a solicitor she met while she was staying in our house. Someone she consulted about her legal position with regard to Harry, her ex. He's a very nice, kind, reliable man.'

'And—and your son?'

'The solicitor has legally adopted him and has told me quite plainly that he will take over the responsibility for him. Tim knows who I am, of course, and we see each other from time to time. But he's had enough father figures in his life, so I make certain that I don't interfere. And I understand that he's to have a brother or sister before too long.'

'So Camilla is happy, then?' Alys was unable to keep an acid note out of her voice.

'Yes, she is. Don't begrudge her that, Alys,' Titus added. 'She's been through a lot. And she was never the trickster you thought her to be.'

Not knowing whether that was true or not, Alys glanced impatiently at the shop. 'Do you think Gail is actually going to buy something?'

'Probably not—unless Jack buys it for her. Let's walk on a little way, shall we?'

Alys hesitated but Titus had already begun to stroll further up the street, so that she had little choice but to follow. A few shops further on they came to a carpet gallery and stood in the doorway to watch two women in traditional dress seated at a loom where they wove the millions of richly coloured silk threads that went into even quite a small carpet. 'No wonder they're so expensive,' Alys remarked, looking at the price labels. 'It must take months to make one of those large carpets.'

Titus didn't answer, and when she glanced towards him Alys found that he wasn't looking in the shop window but towards her. And what she saw in his eyes, in that unguarded moment, made her heart start to race wildly. Naked desire, need, longing; they were all there, in aching intensity. But the next second Titus had looked beyond her and was smiling as Gail walked towards them. One moment Alys had been certain that look was for her, but it had happened so swiftly that now she wasn't sure; maybe it had been Gail that Titus had been looking at, longing for.

'Where's Jack?' Titus asked.

'Oh, he's still in the shop, buying a wallet. He sent me on to find you. They had the most gorgeous leather coat in there,' she told Alys. 'I absolutely loved it, but so expensive! Are you all right, Alys?' she added when she got no reply.

'What? Oh, yes, thanks. Sorry, I—I was miles away.' Which was a huge lie, because Alys's thoughts were entirely on Titus, who was standing only two feet away. He gave her a speculative glance which Alys avoided by walking over to a jewellery shop to look in the window. She had seen Titus in a similar shop back in Santorini, but Gail hadn't flashed any new bracelet or anything, which Alys was quite sure she would have done, so presumably the gift hadn't been for her. So did he have someone else back in England?

Jack rejoined them and they walked further along the street, the two men stopping to have their shoes polished at a stand that even contained a clock, then they found a restaurant near the old caravanserai. Alys found herself in a booth next to Titus and opposite Jack, which she didn't know whether to be pleased or sorry about. She was disturbingly close to Titus, their shoulders and hips almost touching, but at least she didn't have to look him directly in the face. She felt restless and uncertain again, at one moment excited, the next desolate, and all the while trying to appear quite natural.

A smiling waiter came up, brought them aperitifs in very small glasses, and very large menus. For a while it was OK, as they discussed what they would eat, but then Gail suggested they share a *meze*, mixed dish, with side-dishes of mushrooms and prawns. Without thinking, Alys said, 'Titus has never liked prawns.'

There was a short, pregnant silence as three of them realised the import of what she'd said. Jack spoke at once, trying to cover her mistake, but Gail said firmly, 'Just a minute. What did you mean by saying he's "never liked" them, Alys?'

'Er—didn't you say that when we sat together at dinner the other night?' Alys said to Titus, her tone commanding him to agree.

But, 'We've never sat on the same table for dinner on this trip,' Titus answered unhelpfully.

'Lunch, then.'

'Or lunch.' Titus's lips twitched a little at the fuming look Alys gave him, but she nearly died when he turned to Gail and said, 'She knows because we used to live together.'

'Live together?' Gail looked at Alys's flushed cheeks and made the right guess. 'You mean you were lovers?'

'Yes. For quite some time.'

Gail stared at them both, her colour heightening, an angry flare in her eyes. 'And neither of you had the decency to tell me. You both just let me make a fool of myself!'

'No, Gail, that isn't true.' Alys reached out a hand to cover Gail's but the other girl snatched it away. 'Titus and I split up long ago. Until this trip we hadn't seen each other or corresponded, or anything, for a couple of years.' Taking a breath, she said as steadily as she could, 'As far as I'm concerned Titus is completely free to have a relationship with anyone he wants. And I'm— I'm sorry I let him know you'd told me you'd become lovers.'

Gail's chin came up at that and she gave Jack a swift glance, but he was sitting quietly by her side. 'You don't exactly look surprised, Jack. Did—did you know about this?'

'That Alys and Titus had once been close, yes.'

'And—and about me?'

He nodded. 'That, too.'

Gail's face hardened. 'It seems everyone knows everything, then.'

'Not quite.' Titus was looking steadily at Gail. 'I think there's something you have to tell Alys.'

Alys gave him a surprised glance, then suddenly thought, Oh, God, she's going to say that they're engaged. It took a supreme effort to meet Gail's eyes, to wait for her to speak. Gail's mouth looked a little mutinous, but then she shrugged and said, 'Oh, all right.

It wasn't true—what I said about Titus and me. We haven't been to bed together. I made it up,' she finished defiantly, not needing to explain that vanity had made her do it.

'Oh.' Alys could find nothing else to say.

'Well, now that that's all settled, perhaps we can choose what we're going to eat,' Jack said firmly. 'Look, I fancy this red mullet. How about you, Gail?'

Both girls gave him a grateful look, but it would have been difficult to decide whose cheeks were the most flushed. Alys picked up her menu and studied it unseeingly, wondering why Titus had forced poor Gail to admit her lie so openly, why he'd bothered to do it at all. To put the record straight, yes, but for whose benefit? It could only be for Jack or herself, and if it were the former then all Titus need have done was to have a quiet word in Jack's ear. So it was for her own sake, then. But why should he care, unless...? Alys was afraid to think further than that, too scared of having hopes dashed to even think them. Aware that the others were looking at her, she suddenly became very animated, laughing over the menu, chattering about nothing, and stayed that way until, thankfully, the meal was over.

'We still have a couple of hours before the ship sails,' Jack said as they came out of the restaurant. 'What would you like to do?'

'Alys and I are going for a walk along by the sea,' Titus said firmly, adding, so that there would be no mistake, 'We'll see you back at the ship.'

They passed the end of the quay and walked in silence until they'd left the lights of the main town behind, then Titus said, 'Let's go down to the beach.' He jumped down on to the sand and Alys put her hands on his shoulders so that he could lift her down, although she could have jumped easily enough. She took off her shoes and Titus put them in his pockets. He went to take her hand but Alys walked away from him to the edge of the sea. It was a very clear night, the stars sharp in the sky, the moon like polished silver. Titus stood behind her, waiting, until she turned round and said, 'Why?'

'What a question! Which why in particular?'

'Why did you let me go on thinking that you and Gail were lovers?'

'Did it matter so much?'

'You know it damn well mattered!' she exclaimed fiercely. 'Why did you do it? Why did you kiss her so I would see? Was it—was it for revenge?'

'Revenge?'

'Yes, for me deserting you. For my—not coming up to your expectations? The way you described in that sonnet.'

Titus shook his head, hesitated as he found the right words, then said, 'I was furious when you left, devastated that you could do it in such a way, more angry than I've ever felt in my life. I knew that because we'd fallen in love at first sight you regarded our relationship, our lives together, as a dream come true, a perfect romance. I tried to keep it that way for you, but when Camilla and Tim needed me I had no choice but to tell you about them. I didn't want to destroy your dream, Alys, but I had to. And then you spoiled mine by not having a love strong enough to stand by me when I needed you.'

'So it was revenge?'

'No. I went around with Gail and kissed her because I wanted to see how you would react, whether you still cared enough about me to be jealous. It wasn't my idea—

just her vanity which made her brag that we'd gone further than that.'

'And was I suitably jealous?' Alys asked on a bitter note.

'You laughed,' he pointed out shortly. 'So I didn't know what the hell to think. But I definitely knew how I felt when you swam out to sea. I was so worried I was on the point of going in after you to bring you back.'

She didn't comment on that, but said, 'I told you the truth when I said I swam out to be alone.' She was silent for a moment, gazing out to a horizon she couldn't see. 'I was a great disappointment to you, wasn't I?'

But Titus said, 'It was as much my fault; I protected you too much.'

She turned at that, trying to read his face in the soft darkness. 'And I expected too much of you; I wanted your love to be purely for me—even before I met you.'

'A pair of fools, then,' he said gently, and held out his hand.

But again Alys didn't take it, instead saying, 'Why did you proposition me so—so crudely the other night? To make me feel cheap?'

'Of course not,' he said swiftly. 'I still wasn't absolutely sure that you still cared about me. I had to find out.'

'And I suppose my refusing your offer—made you think that I didn't.'

Titus laughed, his voice rich with gentle amusement. 'Of course not; it proved just the opposite. You got furiously, beautifully angry, and I knew for certain that you still loved me. Can you deny it?' She didn't answer and he gave her a tender, amused look. 'Are there any more questions? Because if not——'

'Yes, there are,' Alys surprised him by saying firmly. 'I saw you in a jewellery shop in Santorini, buying something. Who was it for?'

Titus paused, then said, 'A woman named Gwen. I see her several times a week.'

'So there is someone else!' Desperately she tried to keep the devastation out of her voice.

'Yes. She's the woman who comes in to clean the house. Married, and with two grown-up sons. She also has a charm bracelet. I was buying her one to add to it.'

'Oh.'

Coming up to her, Titus put his hands on her shoulders. 'Alys,' he said softly. 'I've missed you so much. Do you know what it's like to lie awake at nights, longing to be with you again?'

'Yes, of course I know,' Alys said brokenly. 'Why didn't you come for me? I waited and waited, but you didn't phone or write, or——'

'Because at first I was so damn angry with you. I felt that we could have sorted it all out if only you'd have listened to me. As soon as Camilla and Tim arrived I packed my things and moved out, just gave them the keys of the house. I did what I had to do and gave them a roof over their heads. But I didn't want to be with *her*; I never have. It was you I wanted.'

'But why didn't you come for me then?'

'I was still flaming mad. You see, you didn't give me a chance to tell you that Tim was ill, that he needed an operation.'

'Ill? Oh, God, Titus, no wonder you were so furious with me.'

He didn't attempt to deny it. 'Yes, well, I saw them through that, but as soon as I could I went to Egypt. I needed time to cool off, to think things through. But while I was there I was offered a post for the next eighteen months. When you didn't answer my letter I decided to take it.'

'You wrote to me?' Alys stared at him in consternation. 'Oh, Titus, I never received it! I swear I didn't. I——'

'I know,' he cut in quickly. 'Your aunt told me. It seems your father was so angry at the way I'd treated you that he just chucked it on the fire.'

'Oh, no! Oh, if only I'd known,' she said in distress.

'Don't blame him, Alys. He thought he was protecting you.'

'What—what did you say, in your letter?'

Titus gave a small shrug. 'Everything that I hoped would bring you back. That it had all been my fault. That I loved you, wanted you, needed you. That I couldn't live without you. And an apology, of course, for not having told you about Camilla and Tim before.'

'It would have been better if you had.'

'Yes,' Titus admitted. 'But it was so long ago, almost forgotten. And the kind of love that we had only comes along once in a thousand lifetimes; I wanted to keep it perfect for you.' He sighed. 'I was wrong. I ruined everything.'

Eager for him not to take all the blame, Alys said, 'No, it was my fault, too. I was possessive and jealous.'

'As I would have been if there had been another man in your life. I've been so afraid that you might have met someone else while I was away.'

Alys laughed shakily. 'And I thought that you had stopped loving me, that you'd grown to hate me.'

'Never that,' he said softly. 'Never, ever that.'

He went to take her in his arms but she put her hands flat against his chest, holding him off, her face a mirror of distress. 'Oh, Titus, it all went so horribly wrong. In just one day! If only you'd told me. If only I'd listened. I thought that you wanted your son more than me. That you would fall in love with Camilla and——'

'Don't be ridiculous,' he said roughly. 'How could I ever love anyone but you?'

She went into his arms then, throwing her own round his neck as he held her tightly, oh, so tightly, as if he would never let her go.

'Oh, Titus, my love. I've been so afraid. When you didn't come for me I thought I'd lost you, that I'd never see you again.'

He kissed her passionately, silencing her doubts. 'I'll never stop loving you, wanting you. You were always in my thoughts, every day, every night.' Alys was laughing, crying, and he kissed away her tears, hugging her in a huge bear-hug, laughing as he held her. 'Oh, my darling girl. We've been such a stubborn pair of fools.'

'But never, never again. Promise me you'll never keep things from me, not even to protect me.'

'Of course.'

She put her hands on either side of his face, gazing up at him with eyes overflowing with love and happiness. Shakily she said, 'And I'll promise not to be a coward in future.'

'You found the courage to stay on the ship.'

'Because in my heart I so wanted this to happen, hoped against hope every minute of the day. And, anyway, I couldn't have left, not when there was the chance of just seeing you, of hearing your voice—even if you were talking to Gail,' Alys admitted. 'Oh, Titus! Hold me. Don't ever let me go.'

'Never again. Never again!' He found her mouth, kissing her compulsively, his shoulders hunching as passion deepened, sending them both into a dizzying whirl of emotion, where roaring need drowned out the noise of the sea, and the fire of desire took the warmth from the night. Titus rained kisses on her eyes, her throat, explored her mouth almost as if it were the first time, but his need was deeper, more urgent than the first time, because now he knew the pleasure that her body could give him, knew that only in their mutual love could there be true sensual perfection.

At last he lifted his head, his breath rasping in his throat, his heart thumping. 'Let's go back to the ship,' he said urgently. 'Let's go *now.*'

Alys laughed a little, her heart beating as crazily as his. 'Oh, *yes*! Yes and yes and yes.'

Her undisguised eagerness made Titus burst into laughter, too, and they stood there on the shore, like a pair of fools, laughing uncontrollably. But then Titus put his arm round her and began to walk her back towards the town, his step brisk. 'Come on.'

'Hey, not so fast,' Alys laughed, but her step was just as eager.

'Are you crazy? I've waited two years for tonight.'

She slowed a little and looked into his face, able to see him now by the light of a lamp-post. Sure of him now but still wanting to hear his answer, she said, 'There hasn't been anyone else?'

'No one. Not Camilla, not Gail. Surely you must know that I couldn't possibly want anyone after what we had?'

Alys smiled and reached up to kiss him, thinking that she would never be unhappy again, but couldn't help saying teasingly, 'Aren't you going to ask me whether or not I met anyone else?'

'Another man?' Titus grinned, a light of triumphant happiness in his eyes—that, and deep, impatient desire.

'I knew you hadn't. Your aunt told me before I came on the cruise that——' He broke off, realising what he'd said. 'Ah! I meant to tell you about that later. You see——'

'I'm beginning to,' Alys interrupted. She drew back a little. 'Are you telling me that you *knew* I'd be on the ship?'

'Well, yes. You see, after I got back to England I immediately tried to find you, but your parents, quite rightly thinking that I'd upset you enough, wouldn't tell me where you were. Then I remembered your aunt and went to see her. It seemed that she was starting to get a bit worried about you, but she wouldn't give me your address either; she said that she felt we ought to meet on neutral ground and that she'd think of something. Then she read about the original lecturer's accident and thought it would give us an ideal opportunity. So she immediately rang me and asked me to apply to go in his place. She guaranteed to get you to come along if I got the job.' He grinned. 'She also said that you wouldn't be able to run away again.'

'Did she indeed?' There was growing indignation in Alys's voice. 'So between you, you—manipulated me into coming on this trip!'

'Only because we both loved you,' Titus said swiftly.

'But when I saw you I did turn and run. Surely that must have made you realise at once that I still cared about you? Why didn't you come right out then and tell me that you loved me and wanted me? Why let me go through all this—this torment of letting me think you were in love with Gail?'

'But I wasn't sure how you felt,' Titus answered urgently. 'OK, I knew that seeing me again had made an impact on you, but it could just as easily have been hate as love. I had to be sure. And your aunt had told me she was afraid that you were sinking into a kind of apathy, that you were hiding yourself away in the school. So I thought that if I made you jealous about Gail then it might shake you out of it, make you start fighting back.'

'I took the job at the school because it was a kind of sanctuary,' Alys said sharply. 'A place where I could lick my wounds... Because your not coming for me hurt like hell! You don't know how much. I wasn't *apathetic*; I was hurting and trying so hard not to show it. And now you've put me through all this again, twisting the knife, making me despair of hope, when all the time you——'

'Alys, I'm sorry. I didn't know. How could I know? Darling, please, let me——'

But she wrenched herself free of his hold and ran ahead of him up the beach to some steps leading to the pavement. But then Alys had to stop and turn. 'Give me my shoes.'

'Alys, please listen. I——'

'No!' She dropped her shoes to the ground and thrust her feet into them. 'I've been going through hell! All the trouble we had before was because you weren't open with me and you're still keeping things from me now.'

'It wasn't like that.' Titus came up the steps and tried to catch hold of her but she pushed him away, arms flailing angrily. 'Keep away from me! If you touch me I'll scream.'

'Don't be ridiculous! All I wanted was for us to be happy, to be sure.'

He took hold of her wrist. Alys opened her mouth and screamed—loudly. Titus cursed and reached out to put his hand over her mouth, but it was too late—already several people were running towards them, shouting. A couple of men caught hold of him, making Titus let her go as he turned to speak to them, to explain. But Alys took the opportunity to hurry away, abandoning him. Let him sort it out! She was still fuming with anger, too furious to care if he got into trouble.

It was quite a long walk back to the ship and at any other time Alys might have felt uneasy walking through a foreign town alone at night, but tonight she strode along so purposefully, her anger so obvious, that any man who wanted to approach her immediately thought better of it and left her strictly alone. Reaching the ship, Alys climbed the gangway, but instead of going to find her aunt to vent her anger on her, too, she paced the length of the ship and back again, wishing there were something violently physical she could do to work out her anger. There wasn't, of course; there was nothing to do but stride the deck, waiting for Titus to come back. Jack and Gail returned, arm in arm, and went off to the bar by the pool for a drink, as did many of the passengers. Midnight came and still Titus hadn't come back. Then, open-mouthed, she saw him being marched along the quay by two policemen! And the cruise director had to go down and vouch for him before the police would let him on board. Serve him right! Alys thought, and went down to her cabin, deciding to make him suffer for at least another day before she forgave him.

By the next morning the whole ship was buzzing with the news of Titus's 'arrest'. He came looking for her early, banging on the cabin door before breakfast.

'Who on earth can that be?' Aunt Lou exclaimed.

'It's Titus,' Alys said calmly. 'Probably worried in case I murdered you for getting together with him behind my back.'

'Oh! So he told you. Does that mean...?' Her aunt looked at her tentatively.

Titus banged on the door again.

'Will you please tell him to go away and leave me alone?'

'Are you quite sure that's what you want me to say?'

'Quite sure,' Alys answered firmly.

Aunt Lou put her head round the door to give him the message, but Titus was waiting in the corridor, leaning against the wall, arms folded, when they came out to go to breakfast. Alys ignored him and walked past. Titus immediately came after her. The corridor was too narrow to walk side by side, so he said forcefully into her ear, 'Would you please explain to the cruise director what happened last night? He's convinced I'm some kind of sex maniac!'

'Too bad!' Alys retorted, enjoying herself.

'Are you going to tell him?'

'No.'

'You're going to pay for this when I get you alone, my love,' Titus told her, a menacing glint in his eyes.

'Threats won't make me change my mind.' But Alys's heart sang with excited anticipation, and she thought that maybe she wouldn't punish him for quite so long after all.

He moved away as they neared the dining-room and Alys and Aunt Lou went to sit at a table with Gail, who was waving madly at them. 'Have you heard about Titus?' she demanded of Alys as soon as they sat down.

'Yes. It was me he had a row with. I'm afraid I left him to get out of it alone.'

'I thought it was probably something like that,' Gail said offhandedly, surprising Alys, who had thought she would have been more interested. But Gail leaned towards her and said, 'Imagine! When I got to my cabin last night I found that gorgeous leather coat I told you about, the one that cost the earth. Jack must have bought it and had them send it to the ship. Wasn't that sweet of him?' She frowned. 'You know, I really like Jack. He's good fun. Not at all boring. And there's nothing *intense* about him. Do you know what I mean?' Alys nodded and Gail gave a regretful sigh. 'It's such a pity he hasn't any money; I feel I could be comfortable with him.'

Alys didn't say anything, but after breakfast she sought out the woman who'd told them about Jack being a consultant. 'Do you know Mrs Turnbull?' she asked, pointing Gail out. 'She was telling us about a relative who has an illness that's beaten all the doctors. I wondered, if you told her about your sister...'

'Oh, of course. I'll go and tell her at once.'

'Er—she did sort of tell me in confidence, so if you could just bring it up in conversation,' Alys suggested.

'Of course. I *quite* understand.'

Alys walked away, grinning to herself, thinking that she'd done her good deed for the day.

But there she was wrong. The ship was sailing through the scattered islands off the Turkish coast, islands that belonged to Greece. Some of them were very small and uninhabited but others had long golden beaches and were popular holiday islands. Because the ship was small it could go closer in to the shore, giving the passengers a better view, the officer at the bridge giving the names of the islands and towns they passed over the loudspeaker from the bridge. They rounded the rocky headland of one of the islands—and found a pedalo with three young boys on board immediately in their path.

There was little the helmsman could do. Shouts of alarm came vividly over the loudspeaker and everyone rushed to the side. The siren sounded a furious warning but the two seated children panicked, both trying to turn different ways. The third boy, who had been standing up behind them, slipped, hit his head on the edge of the seat and fell into the sea. Alys kicked off her shoes, climbed the rail, and dived cleanly in.

Her biggest fear was the ship's propeller, making her swim fast to the pedalo. The boys had got it together now but were looking into the sea for their friend.

'Get going! I'll find him,' Alys yelled, and waved them away.

The ship was very close now, only yards away. She dived deep, thankful that the water was so clear, and found the boy almost at once. He was coming to, struggling to get back to the surface. Grabbing him, Alys put her hand over his mouth and nose, taking him deeper down. He struggled at first, and it took all her strength to hold him, but then he grew still. Overhead there was a great roaring sound which was gradually silenced as the ship's engines were stopped, but it took a while for the blades to slow and become still. The roaring went on but it was in Alys's head, in her tightening chest as she strove to hold her breath. She kept her eyes on the bottom of the ship and, as soon as the screws stopped, shot up to the surface, going fast, afraid for the boy, but her arms aching and feeling very weak now.

They broke through to the blessed air, and suddenly Titus was there, taking the boy from her, giving him mouth-to-mouth while he held him. Alys sank back under the water, exhausted, felt Titus grab her and pull her up. 'Hold on to my shoulders.'

She got behind him, put her arms round his neck and closed her eyes, floating, letting life gradually creep back into her limbs. Dimly, she became aware that a boat was being lowered from the ship, that the two other boys were miraculously OK on the pedalo, that people had seen from the distant beach and another boat was putting out from there.

'Hang on,' Titus said urgently. 'Just a little while.'

'I'm all right. The boy?'

'I think he's breathing.'

The boats picked them up, took them back to the shore. They sat together in one, Titus's arms close around her, while Jack worked on the boy in another, and again stood together on the beach, waiting, a little apart from the crowd that had gathered, until the boy was taken away in an ambulance. After seeing him off, Jack came over to them and gave a thumbs-up sign. 'He's fine. Crying for his mother. How about you two?'

'We're OK.' Titus grinned. 'In every way.' And his arm tightened.

'Glad to hear it. You've certainly given the passengers something to talk about. We'd better get back to the ship.'

'Titus?' Alys gave him an appealing look. 'Do we have to go back? I've had enough of that cruise.'

He gave a sigh of relief. 'Thank goodness for that. I'm sick to death of that damn boat! Jack, do you think you could persuade them to get our things together and bring them ashore?'

'Of course. No trouble.'

Alys said, 'Please apologise to Aunt Lou—and tell her it worked. She'll understand.'

Jack went off in the ship's boat and Titus grinned at her. 'Have you any idea where we are?'

'No. Does it matter?'

'Not in the least.'

'Maybe there'll be a little house we can rent for a week or so.'

Titus bent to kiss her. 'I think we'll need it for longer than that.'

'A month or so, then.'

'I don't have to be back until October,' he pointed out.

Alys chuckled richly. 'But I have to be back in September.'

'I'm afraid they'll have to get along without you, my darling. Because by then you'll not only be married but pregnant.'

'Will I indeed? Is that a threat?'

'No, my dearest love. That is a promise.' Titus took her in his arms to seal the promise with a kiss, and the cheers of the passengers still lining the rails of the ship echoed enthusiastically across the water.

POSTCARDS FROM EUROPE

HARLEQUIN PRESENTS®

Hi—

The sun was shining brightly here in Spain until I met Felipe de Santis. The man is used to giving orders and doesn't respect my abilities as a journalist. But I'm going to get my story—and I'm going to help Felipe's sister!

Love, Maggie

P.S. If only I could win Felipe's love....

Travel across Europe in 1994 with Harlequin Presents. Collect a new Postcards From Europe title each month!

Don't miss
DARK SUNLIGHT
by Patricia Wilson
Harlequin Presents #1644

Available in April, wherever Harlequin Presents books are sold.

HARLEQUIN®

Don't miss these Harlequin favorites by some of our most distin-
guished authors!
And now, you can receive a discount by ordering two or more titles!

HT#25409	THE NIGHT IN SHINING ARMOR by JoAnn Ross	$2.99	☐
HT#25471	LOVESTORM by JoAnn Ross	$2.99	☐
HP#11463	THE WEDDING by Emma Darcy	$2.89	☐
HP#11592	THE LAST GRAND PASSION by Emma Darcy	$2.99	☐
HR#03188	DOUBLY DELICIOUS by Emma Goldrick	$2.89	☐
HR#03248	SAFE IN MY HEART by Leigh Michaels	$2.89	☐
HS#70464	CHILDREN OF THE HEART by Sally Garrett	$3.25	☐
HS#70524	STRING OF MIRACLES by Sally Garrett	$3.39	☐
HS#70500	THE SILENCE OF MIDNIGHT by Karen Young	$3.39	☐
HI#22178	SCHOOL FOR SPIES by Vickie York	$2.79	☐
HI#22212	DANGEROUS VINTAGE by Laura Pender	$2.89	☐
HI#22219	TORCH JOB by Patricia Rosemoor	$2.89	☐
HAR#16459	MACKENZIE'S BABY by Anne McAllister	$3.39	☐
HAR#16466	A COWBOY FOR CHRISTMAS by Anne McAllister	$3.39	☐
HAR#16462	THE PIRATE AND HIS LADY by Margaret St. George	$3.39	☐
HAR#16477	THE LAST REAL MAN by Rebecca Flanders	$3.39	☐
HH#28704	A CORNER OF HEAVEN by Theresa Michaels	$3.99	☐
HH#28707	LIGHT ON THE MOUNTAIN by Maura Seger	$3.99	☐

Harlequin Promotional Titles

#83247	YESTERDAY COMES TOMORROW by Rebecca Flanders	$4.99	☐
#83257	MY VALENTINE 1993	$4.99	☐
	(short-story collection featuring Anne Stuart, Judith Arnold, Anne McAllister, Linda Randall Wisdom)		

(limited quantities available on certain titles)

	AMOUNT	$
DEDUCT:	10% DISCOUNT FOR 2+ BOOKS	$
ADD:	POSTAGE & HANDLING	$
	($1.00 for one book, 50¢ for each additional)	
	APPLICABLE TAXES*	$ _____
	TOTAL PAYABLE	$ _____
	(check or money order—please do not send cash)	

To order, complete this form and send it, along with a check or money order for the
total above, payable to Harlequin Books, to: **In the U.S.:** 3010 Walden Avenue,
P.O. Box 9047, Buffalo, NY 14269-9047; **In Canada:** P.O. Box 613, Fort Erie, Ontario,
L2A 5X3.

Name: _____

Address: _____ City: _____

State/Prov.: _____ Zip/Postal Code: _____

*New York residents remit applicable sales taxes.
Canadian residents remit applicable GST and provincial taxes.

HBACK-JM

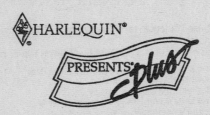